Green Street in Black and White

A Chicago Story

Dave Larsen

For more information and further discussion, visit

ReformedJournal.com

ISBN: 978-1-64180-216-1

Version 1.0

Cover design by Rick Nease. RickNeaseArt.com

Author photo by Alyssa McElheny.

Published by Reformed Journal Books
Publishing services by Front Edge Publishing
42807 Ford Road, No. 234
Canton, MI, 48187

For my parents, Alf and Marion, and sister Karen,
who lived and loved through it all.

Not everything that is faced can be changed, but nothing can be changed until it is faced.

James Baldwin

Children have never been very good at listening to their elders, but they have never failed to imitate them.

James Baldwin

You can observe a lot by watching.

Yogi Berra

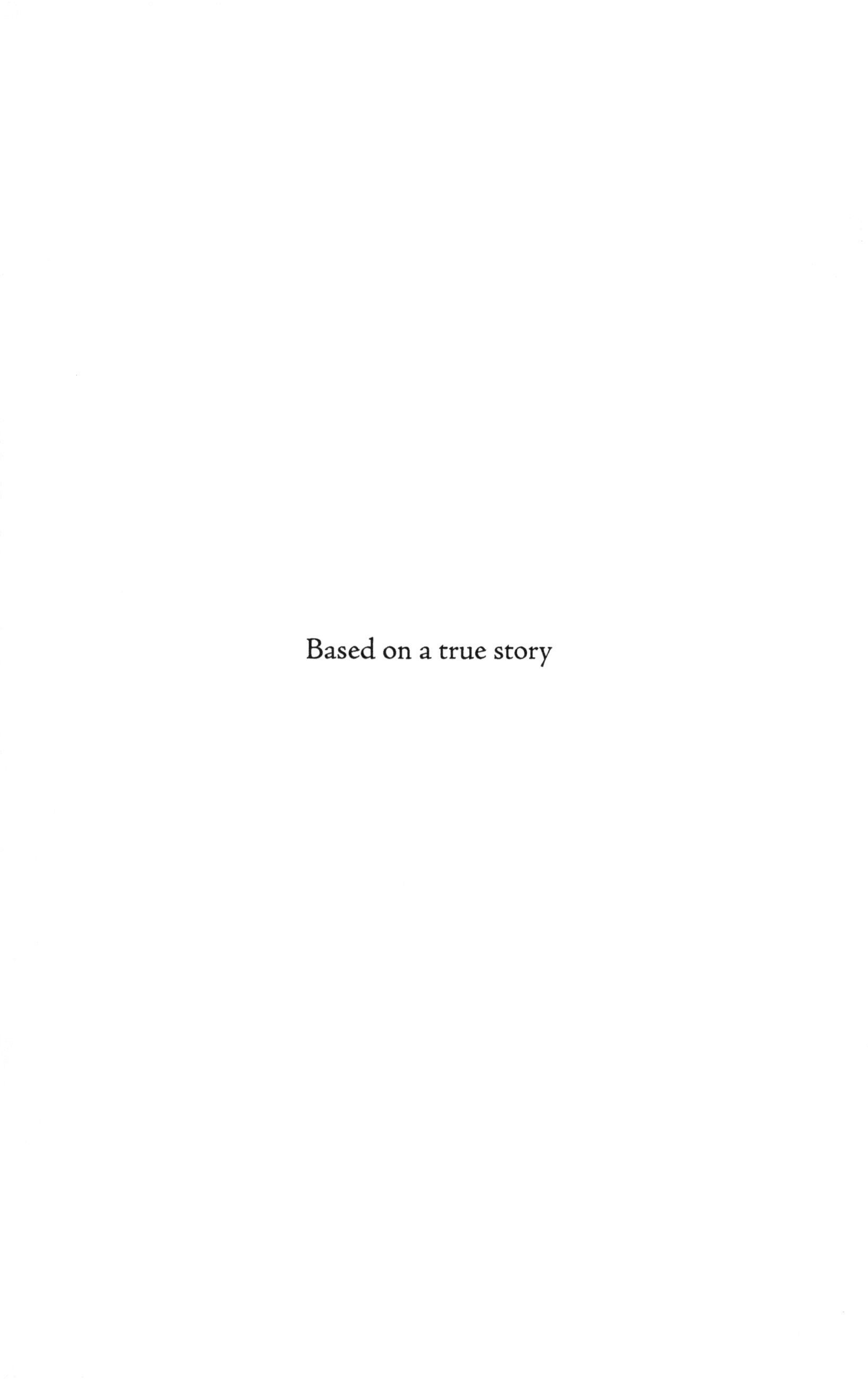

Based on a true story

One

"I think I'm going to burst!"

Frank Bertolli looked back and grimaced as he hustled across the street toward Old Man Finnegan's front porch.

Frank, aka Catholic Frank, aka Francis A. Sissy, was mercilessly picked on by the other members of the Green Street Boys. His crime was simple: he was an idolatrous papist. If pressed, none of the Green Street Boys could actually define that term, but it didn't matter. They'd heard their parents whisper those words and knew they made Frank different. Plus, Frank had thick black glasses and a squeaky voice. Worse yet, he was in love with Annette Funicello.

All the Green Street Boys admired Annette's perky breasts, but what chance did Frank have with her? He had the good looks of Alfred E. Neuman.

Still, he was a Green Street Boy, and initiation into the Green Street Boys was renewed annually. Today was Frank's turn. An hour earlier, he'd drunk a quart of Pepsi. Now, as the overhead roar of a plane approaching Midway Airport provided cover, he pulled aside the loose lattice work beneath Old Man Finnegan's front porch and quietly squeezed under, being careful not to bump his head on the wood above. Taking a long leak under Old Man Finnegan's porch was the first step in the initiation process.

Erik, Eddie, and Pete, the other Green Street Boys, hid behind parked cars in front of the Clements' house, across the street from Old Man Finnegan's, keeping watch.

Old Man Finnegan was the neighborhood grouch, a widower with all the charm of a soiled sock. Rumor had it he parked a shotgun just inside his front door and wouldn't hesitate to use it on trespassers caught desecrating his property. Taking a long leak under his porch was akin to tango dancing through a minefield, and each of the Green Street Boys had imagined emerging from under the porch to find Old Man Finnegan in his flannel shirt, greasy jeans, and dirty red suspenders aiming that shotgun directly at him.

After a minute, Frank rolled out from under the porch grinning and ran toward the others. They ran back across the street and climbed onto the Pedersens' porch, where the Green Street Boys hung out on summer days.

"I feel ten thousand times better," Frank said.

Everybody had a front porch, a place to escape the summer heat. Nobody had air conditioning—unless you were some hoity-toity on the Magnificent Mile or in a mansion on the North Shore. Green Street had front porches, God's air conditioning, and though adults ruled their porches after supper, the Pedersen porch belonged to the Green Street Boys during summer days.

The Green Street Boys didn't have a hierarchy, but by virtue of meeting on his front porch, the club belonged to Erik Pedersen. Erik split summer vacation between the front porch and the treehouse his father Magnus had built in the three-pronged fork of a backyard maple. Magnus had secured a section of discarded plywood from the alley behind the house to serve as a platform and had nailed steps cut from a two-by-four to the side of the tree. A pail on a pulley held whatever Erik was reading at the time—biographies of heroic figures like Daniel Boone or Robin Hood, a Sherlock Holmes mystery from the local public library, the latest edition of Marvel comics, or a smuggled *Mad* magazine. The treehouse was for reading and spying, and on his plywood perch, leaning against the thick branch of the maple and devoted to whatever the pail held, Erik visited other worlds. On most summer days he would ascend and wait for his father to come home from work—unless the porch called to him for a Green Street Boys adventure. The Pedersen porch was not very big, just large enough for hanging out and observing. This afternoon it was full of the Green Street Boys.

After they'd caught their breath, Pete said, "You know what comes next, Francis."

Frank squirmed as Pete pulled a jackknife out of his pants pocket. They all held out their middle fingers. Pete pricked Erik and Eddie's fingers, and Frank stuck his middle finger up, flipping the others off.

"I don't wanna," he said.

"You're such a little girl," Pete said.

"I am not," Frank said.

"C'mon, Frank, we're bleeding here."

"Stand still," Pete said as he grabbed Frank's hand and cut his finger. Frank almost started to cry, but held it together as Pete then cut open his own finger. The Green Street Boys stuck their fingers together. They were blood brothers for another summer.

"What are we going to do now?" Frank asked, sucking the blood off his finger.

"Game of war," Pete said. A Dutch immigrant who looked old beyond his years, Pete Koning was the biggest and strongest of the bunch. "Followed by knucks. How 'bout it?"

Their games were often brought to a manly conclusion by knucks. Losers made a fist, extended their arm, and the winner got to whack the others' knuckles with the edge of a full deck of cards, as hard as the winner could muster. The first to bleed was the Big-Time All-Star Girlie Loser. Frank hated knucks.

"I don't wanna play knucks," Frank said.

"Well I do, Francis A. Sissy," Pete said.

"Not today," Erik said. "It's already amazing we got this far without Frank crying. Knucks would be too much. My mom's inside and she'd hear him and then I'd have too much explaining to do."

"I don't cry," Frank said. "Quit making things up."

"You do too!" Eddie Medema said. A slim kid who knew how to leverage his stroke, Eddie was the most forceful knucker among the Green Street Boys. "You cry more than Annette ever has. You almost cried just now when Pete cut your finger. I saw your lip quivering."

"It was not!" Frank said.

"It's a miracle you didn't wet your pants at Finnegan's," Eddie said.

"It's a miracle he went to Finnegan's," Pete said. Pete rose, looked at Eddie and Erik and said, "Maybe we should just take turns punching Frank."

"Stop picking on me." Frank screwed up his face, tightened his lips, clenched his fists, searched for just the right words, and raised his whiny voice. "Shut up, n——!" he shouted.

Erik looked at Pete. Pete looked at Eddie. All three then stared at Frank with open mouths, stunned.

"What did you say?"

"You heard me."

Cursing was one thing, reserved for special occasions far from parental earshot, but a word like this crossed the boundaries of swearing, the norms that governed what did or did not give offense. This was a weapon. Most of the swear words in the Boys' vocabulary brought them together. They were words friends said for a thrill, for laughter, or daring. This was different.

The n-word had never been spoken by any of the Green Street Boys—although all the boys heard it from adults when they weren't supposed to be listening. They knew the word was demeaning and belittling, yet they never threw it at each other. They had other words that did the job. This one carried power way beyond the normal names they called each other: Erik was "Bones" because he was skinny, "Schnozz" stuck to Pete because of his bent, large nose, and Eddie was "Bucky" because of his teeth. But this word stunned. It was meant to mark someone as less than human. They felt it.

"Got your attention, didn't I?" Frank said. "I'm sick of being the big joke all the time. Sick of it. Enough's enough." He stomped his foot, sniveled, hitched up his sagging jeans, and marched down the stairs, heading home. He didn't look back.

A stronger word didn't exist in their neighborhood. It was part of the glossary of the neighborhood, a tool of division, an emblem of hate, and one of their own had introduced it among the Green Street Boys.

Most people in Englewood, as in many Chicago neighborhoods, sought refuge on their porches at night because it brought a sense of calm to the surroundings, a still, enduring center for an increasingly confusing and tense world. The neighborhood noise of the day quieted and gathering in view of your neighbors seemed the most natural thing to do. It was a place and time to check in with each other to see what the day had delivered.

You could almost predict what would be said, and by whom, on the front porches of Englewood. A few years earlier, during the summer of 1959, when the White Sox took the pennant and

Nellie Fox and Luis Aparicio were instant celebrities, housewives ventured their opinions about the chances for a World Series without regard to their husbands' heavily researched predictions. The night the Hitless Wonders beat Cleveland to reach the World Series everyone on Green Street sat on their front porches with their radios tuned in and turned up in unison. Anyone standing in the middle of the street could have clearly heard the play-by-play. Between innings, Green Street echoed with the familiar drumbeat of the Hamm's Beer commercial: "From the land of sky blue waters." When the last batter hit a ground ball to Aparicio, who then stepped on second and started a double play, there was cheering and shouting, followed by the noise of the fire sirens Commissioner Quinn had ordered alive. That summer, the summer of 1959, the White Sox were the talk of every porch on Chicago's South Side.

This summer, the summer of 1962, was different. This was the summer of the n-word. It was spoken often, not only on Green Street, but throughout Englewood, and not just by Frank Bertolli.

Two

Every evening, the Bensemas, who lived in a frame house across from the Pedersens on the west side of Green Street, were always the first to settle on their porch. Supper dishes washed and laid to rest, newspaper sports section in hand, Carl led his wife and two boys to their porch and waited for the neighbors to make their appearances. It was a source of Bensema pride that they were first to their porch. Their unimpressed neighbors knew the Bensemas had little else going for them. Carl was a man of many grievances, ready to unload on anyone who might listen. His sense of personal injustice and long list of complaints fueled his sullen demeanor. According to Carl, he'd been taken advantage of at his job at the Pullman yard, and now, with his red face clenched like a fist, Carl would tell anyone who listened that the neighborhood was going to hell in a hand basket. Carl had all the subtlety of a bazooka.

Florence Bensema longed for a pleasant conversation on the porch with her husband, but it rarely happened. When he wasn't griping about work or the neighborhood, Carl griped about the White Sox. Since she wasn't interested in Jungle Jim

Rivera, Sherman Lollar, or Early Wynn, there was little to talk about. Maybe if Florence had chosen to learn about the White Sox, things might have opened up, but baseball didn't matter to her. And her daily life at home didn't matter much to Carl.

Their two boys—Carl Junior and Richard—were too young for the Green Street Boys, and kept to themselves, never saying much, fearing the disapproval of their father. Life on the Bensema porch was quiet, stifling, and still. So, Florence Bensema pinned her hopes on the arrival of the neighbors, a summer evening ritual that chased the loneliness of her marriage, if only for a few hours.

The Clements, whose house was next to the Bensemas, were also on their small porch each night. They would wait for the Pedersen family to show across the street, since the Bensemas were so dull and conversations rare. The Pedersens would wave and walk over for a chat. Most every afternoon, George Clement would stop for a bump at Donegan's Tavern, and he appreciated that the Pedersens let him cut through their yard on the way. Nothing like a short cut to build a friendship.

George Clement had been retired for six years, yet often wondered why. He had been a welder for the Rock Island Railroad and would go back to the train yard three, maybe four times a week to show his pals how well retired life was treating him. They humored him, aware that they, too, might need some company when they reached the paradise of retirement. George's sooty welder's uniform had been exchanged for a white sleeveless undershirt, Bermuda shorts, and black knee socks above tan corduroy slippers. His curly chest hair fell like a bristly gray and white waterfall over the scoop in his undershirt. George was the patriarch of the Green Street block, the pioneer who had lived there the last thirty-three years. The neighborhood kids loved this tall, whitehaired man whose thick eyebrows danced when he spoke. Erik Pedersen got to know him better than most because of George's late afternoon strolls through their yard on the way home from Donegan's.

Born and raised four blocks from his Green Street home, George met and courted tiny Millie Sheehan when they were both seventeen. They married a year later and then, on their tenth wedding anniversary, bought the white frame bungalow on Green Street which became the center of their universe. They could walk to St. Ignace for mass, National Tea on Halsted for groceries, Donegan's for stimulation, and Sears and Roebuck's on 63rd Street when George needed new slippers. They never had children—couldn't, they were told—so their children were the kids from the neighborhood who came to their porch for stories and cookies and, for the older boys, a racy joke if Millie wasn't in earshot.

The Pedersens had lived on Green Street for two years, moving from a tight apartment two blocks away. While a stretch financially, it was a step up with more space, and they knew that within a few years both Fenna and Magnus would bring two incomes to the cause. Fenna was a nurse who had stepped away from her hospital job to be at home with Erik and his sister, Kristen, until they reached junior high school. Magnus Pedersen worked downtown as the office manager of a mattress company and commuted on the Chicago Transit Authority bus, which ran hot in the summer, cold in the winter, and late almost every day.

Once Fenna washed the dishes after supper and Erik and Kristen picked them up out of the porcelain sink and dried them, the Pedersens waited to go out to the porch until Magnus emerged from his post-supper sanctuary and private retreat on his "throne." With a quick rap on the door and just the right edge to her voice, Fenna would say, "Magnus! Did you fall in?" They would hear the newspaper fold once, then twice, and the familiar reply, "You're ready already?" from inside, as a cigarette (Magnus thought no one knew) was extinguished and flushed. He always claimed he was working on the crossword puzzle.

Erik could relate to his dad's use of the bathroom for clandestine purposes and would occasionally sneak his mother's nursing textbooks off the living room bookshelf for quick peeks at the drawings and diagrams of the female anatomy, a growing interest of his. He was more than a little interested in the Eck sisters, who lived next door, and was always careful not to linger with a nursing book too long on the toilet. He didn't want to arouse suspicion, especially from Kristen, who would snitch to their parents in a heartbeat. There was a lot to learn: sometimes dirty jokes told on the porch, most often by Pete Koning, went so far over Erik's head he hoped he wouldn't be quizzed about the punchline. He learned to laugh on cue (but not too much) and explored the medical drawings and sketches to improve his literacy.

The toilet flush and Magnus's presence in the hallway were the cues for Erik and Kristen to carry the chrome-framed, pink-and-black-speckled vinyl cushioned chairs from the kitchen to the porch, so their parents would not have to sit on the hard concrete stoop.

Green Street was an ethnic patchwork, like the rest of Englewood, a blend of backgrounds and stories and dreams that came to roost in this mix of frame and brick bungalows and two-flats. The Dutch settled here first, and fruitfully. They were farmers and immigrants who moved from Chicago's old west side shortly after the Civil War. Then came the Irish, who were also fruitful. Both established churches and schools and laid claim to the neighborhood as their own. Other ethnicities came, but never in large numbers: Germans, Italians, and a few Scandinavians like Magnus. By 1960, ninety thousand people lived in the three square miles of Englewood.

The Dutch joked about the Irish and the Irish joked about the Dutch. Together, they laughed at the Italians. They laughed easily and were united more because of what they were not, instead of what they were. They were not rich. They were not dirt poor. And especially, they were not Black.

Historically, approximately eighty percent of Chicago real estate had been covered by neighborhood "covenants" which said that "No part of said premises shall be sold, given, conveyed, or leased to any Negro or Negroes." As a result, the Black population, which came to Chicago during the Great Migration, had been packed into an area south of the Loop known as the "Black Belt." Now, the construction of expressways meant thousands had to relocate (conveniently, the expressway curved around Mayor Daley's neighborhood), and with the outlawing of covenants in the 1950s, more and more Black families moved south and west into Englewood. Halsted Street, a north-south thoroughfare, had served as the dividing line in Englewood, with Blacks to the east and whites to the west. That changed in the summer of 1962.

As a result, evening porch talk in Englewood was typically a variation on a theme: the impending invasion of the Blacks. Conversations mixed fact and fiction, rumor and fear. On the night of the day that Frank Bertolli had shocked the Green Street Boys with the n-word, Carl Bensema walked off his porch and joined the Pedersens, Clements, Ecks, and Konings, who were talking in front of the Pedersen house. "Listen, neighbors," Carl said, "I hear that some of them have moved west of Hamilton Park. My cousin told me yesterday." Hamilton Park was four blocks east of Green Street. There was no question who he meant by "them."

"Don't surprise me," Werner Eck said. "It won't be long now."

"Wanna hear a great story?" Henk Koning said. "I just heard about what happened at the barber shop on 71st, you know,

Kelly's place, on the north side next to the shoe repair. One of them strolled in to get a haircut and shave. So, get this. Old Kelly takes out his razor, slaps it back and forth on the strop a dozen times and tells the colored guy he's never given a shave to his kind. 'Hope this turns out ok,' he says. And the guy whips off the cloth and runs out the door. Turned pale, they said."

Everyone laughed and Carl Bensema started up again. "It's not safe anymore around here, especially by Hamilton Park. Stuff like purse snatchings and beatings if you're too close to where they are. I tell my kids to stay away."

Magnus looked at Carl quizzically. Carl's kids weren't old enough to go by themselves to Hamilton Park. "Think I'm going to sit for a while and enjoy the breeze," Magnus said, taking Fenna's hand and walking back onto their porch.

Carl kept talking. "Look, here's the deal. The fact is that if you don't sell your place soon enough you get stuck and your property value goes way down. You talk to any realtor and that's what they'll say."

Magnus let Carl's words fall as he walked away, and settled in for the evening. After a while, the new streetlights, Mayor Daley's pride, came on and he noticed most of his neighbors had abandoned their porches for the night. He was just about to head in when a car came down Green Street and stopped in front of the Clement house. George Clement greeted the driver at his front door and welcomed him inside.

Magnus had an idea about who might be coming to the Clement house so late. He and Erik stayed on their porch in the shadows and after a while George and the man came outside. Their conversation drifted across the street. "Thanks for staying up for this, Mr. Clement," the visitor said. "These days, we often work in the dark. It's just safer this way."

They shook hands and the man went to the trunk of his car. After slowly looking around, he lifted a thin rectangular sign out of his trunk, a sign that was to change so much for so many that summer. The man put the metal sign into the small plot of grass in front of the Clement house and he and George shook hands once more.

Magnus took his son inside without a word.

The next morning, the rest of the block saw what Magnus and Erik had seen across the street the night before. George and Millie had had enough. Their house was for sale.

When the Green Street Boys gathered on the Pedersen porch that morning, Erik rehearsed the drama of the night before. The Boys walked together across the street to see the sign up close for themselves. White letters on a red background gave the phone number to Regal Realtors. The words 'For Sale' stood in the center.

"This is the real deal, guys," Frank said, rubbing the sign with his hands. "You just watch the dominoes fall now."

"Go soak your head, Frank," Pete said. "What do you know about this stuff anyway?

Frank didn't respond. He knew he was right.

Three

The Green Street Boys weren't the only ones fascinated by the For Sale sign on the Clements' lawn. The rectangular tin structure, with its large white letters on a red background, shouted for attention. Word passed up and down the street and some even walked over when they went out to pick up their morning *Tribune* to see what the fuss was about. Yet no one climbed the steps to the Clements' porch to ask why.

The sign was more or less expected. The Clements were different people than they had been a few weeks earlier. Things had changed on a breezy Friday afternoon when George took his ritual walk for a drink at Donegan's and then stopped to pick up the afternoon *Daily News* at National Tea. George was a creature of habit, and his afternoon routine was as predictable as an alderman's broken promise.

He arrived at Donegan's before the other regulars got off work because he fancied himself the unofficial host of the place. It was his self-appointed function to greet everyone as they came in and detect any sullen spirit before gloom spread through the joint. The inside of the tavern was dark and gloomy enough already, the bar of dark wood and the tin ceiling coated with dust and grime. George had a seat near the door at the corner of the bar to divert anyone with the blues before they killed the mood.

"Hey Barney, how they hangin'?" he said. "Give the missus a peck for me." He took a sip, looked around and said, "Tommy lad, what's with the new cap? Birthday or somethin'?" George knew everybody at Donegan's and was always ready to listen—he was their father confessor if the bartender was otherwise occupied or the parish priest not to their liking. He saw another of the regulars walk in. "Now Mikey, I think you owe me a fiver from the bet last week. Just buy me a couple beers and we're even."

George looked at his watch and saw it was 5:15, which meant it was time to leave and pick up the *Daily News* at National Tea before heading home. From Donegan's, he cut across Halsted to the grocery store. The large building with the picture windows full of neatly stacked canned goods and packages was no longer the center of debate it had been when it opened two years earlier. National Tea was one of those new chains that threatened the mom and pop grocery stores scattered throughout Chicago's neighborhoods. It offered regular sales, coupons, S&H Green Stamps, and, controversially, was open on Sunday. National Tea even boasted a parking lot, which meant shoppers could drive from other neighborhoods and load up, putting more in a car trunk than one could ever put in the flatbed of a red Radio Flyer wagon or grocery stroller.

George always cut through the short stretch of alley between Halsted and Green Street that ran from the National Tea parking lot to the back gate of the Pedersens' home. Erik Pedersen would most likely be perched on the backyard tree platform Magnus had built. From his perch, he might catch a glimpse of one of the radiant Eck sisters on their second-floor back porch, watch the ragman ply his trade as he went from house to house in the alley, or even spot a member of his church coming out of the back door of the fortune-telling place on Halsted. But, most importantly, this was the best vantage point from which to see the CTA bus coming down Halsted bringing Magnus home. His dad would come off the bus carrying his smart leather briefcase with a newspaper tucked under his arm.

This Friday afternoon, it looked to Erik like Mr. Clement had had a particularly good time at Donegan's. There was a spring to his step, and Erik could hear George's customary whistle, a bit louder and livelier than usual. George was about to grab the gate and swing it open when he was stopped by three Black kids, a bit older than Erik, who stepped out from behind O'Sullivan's garage next door.

Halsted Street was the Maginot Line of the neighborhood, and it was unusual to see Black people on this side of it. From the tree, Erik could see George was surprised and heard him say, "Afternoon, boys." He and the three kids stood as still as settled concrete. "You from around here?"

"It don't matter, old man," the tallest said. "You got any cigarettes?"

George began to speak but had no time to answer. One of the kids took a quick step from behind the tallest and swung a baseball bat into the side of George's head. George fell instantly, first against the gate and then onto the concrete alley, groaning, as the other two rolled him over and searched the pockets of his Bermuda shorts. His newspaper blew in the air, scattering down the alley page by page, and Erik froze at the swiftness of the assault.

"Shit! Not much here!" the tall one said angrily, landing a hard kick to George's side. George moaned and tucked his legs to his substantial belly. Erik could see blood coming from the side of George's head where the Louisville Slugger had connected.

Not sure what he should or could do, Erik stood in the crotch of the tree and yelled, "Hey, let him go! Go on, before I call the cops!"

The attackers froze momentarily, looking around for the voice up in the air. Taking stock of the skinny kid in a tree, they laughed, and the tall one shot back, "You come down, Zacchaeus, and do your business with us. You be smart, you keep your skinny white ass up that tree."

Zacchaeus? A name from Sunday School at a time like this? But, like Zacchaeus, Erik came down, sliding down the rickety slat steps nailed to the side of the tree before jumping the final three feet.

Looking up as his feet hit the ground, Erik spotted a green and cream CTA bus slowing down on Halsted and could hear the brakes as it stopped. His father would be stepping off that bus on his way to the alley where Mr. Clement lay bleeding. Erik felt he needed to do something before his dad showed up and became part of the mess in the alley.

"You ... you don't scare me," Erik said. "I'm doing it. I'm calling the cops. Get the hell out of here! Now!" He hardly believed he'd actually said the word "hell." The only other time he had said that word was in church when reciting the Apostle's Creed. But this seemed like the right time to say it. Mr. Clement moved and moaned again from the concrete. Erik's voice was still a tone north of puberty, and the attackers looked at him instead of George Clement.

"C'mon! C'mon! You want this? You're next, dumbass." The tall one gripped the back gate and began to swing it open with one hand. In the other he flashed a switchblade, shiny and persuasive and frightening. Switchblades were the stuff of legend, of gang mystique, and Green Street Boys porch talk. It looked nothing like the puny pocketknife Pete used for Green Street Boys initiations.

Erik was about to spin on his heels and make a rapid retreat when he heard a voice behind him. His mother was on the bottom step of the back-porch stoop, shouting at the boys and waving a spatula above her head. "Seriously!? What is she doing?" Erik thought, watching his slender apron-clad mother.

Magnus Pedersen turned the corner into the alley and stopped, quickly absorbing the incongruous scene, and then threw his hard-shell leather briefcase straight into the stomach of one of the attackers.

"Hey, get outta here! Leave him alone. Go on. Get outta here!" His tone was firm and confident, as insistent as if he were chasing a rabbit from his vegetable garden. The element of surprise, his sudden approach, Fenna's deadly spatula, and the possibility of the police arriving convinced the attackers to move on. They ran into the National Tea lot and split in three directions when they reached Halsted.

Fenna knelt over George and then sent Erik to the house to call an ambulance and the police, in that order. George was conscious, but barely. Fenna bandaged George's head with her apron and kept talking to him as his face drained of color. Magnus sent Kristen to fetch Millie Clement.

The police arrived before the ambulance, and their sirens attracted a crowd. Sixteen-year-old Doris Eck, the prettiest of the Eck sisters, came out. This was the closest Erik had ever been to her. Every so often she would come out the back door with a chair and book in hand, in her short shorts, stretch her lovely long legs over the porch railing, and toss her curly black hair over her shoulders. Erik would stare from his treehouse under the brim of his baseball cap.

She had cut-off jean shorts on today, and Erik was taking in those long tanned legs and wondering if she'd ever notice him, wondering how old he'd have to be so the four-year difference in their ages wouldn't matter, when he started to feel guilty about staring at her while George lay wounded.

Carl Bensema joined the crowd, out of breath from running toward the commotion. He pushed his way to the inner circle and said, "I bet they were colored." Magnus turned and glared at Carl.

Pete Koning rolled up on his bike, leaned it against the fence, and took in the situation. He made his way to Erik and whispered, "Whatsup?" Erik, still looking at Doris Eck's legs while thinking he really ought to be more focused on George, didn't respond.

Frank Bertolli wedged his way in and felt a hand on his shoulder. He looked and saw the greasy jeans, flannel shirt, and red suspenders of Old Man Finnegan. "Damn coward," Old Man Finnegan said. Frank swallowed hard.

"I'm sorry, Mr. Finnegan," he stammered. He was about to say something about the other guys forcing him to pee under his porch, but Old Man Finnegan interrupted him. "Whoever did this is a damn coward." Frank stopped talking.

Kristen held Millie's hand as she ushered her through the crowd toward Fenna, who rose and hugged her neighbor. "He'll be all right Millie," Fenna said. "Right now, it looks worse than it is. Head wounds tend to bleed a lot."

Millie knelt next to George, cradling his head with Fenna's now bloody apron.

"Sweetie, George honey, you'll be ok. Fenna says it looks worse than it is." Millie smoothed her wrinkled hand over George's forehead, a warm soft touch in contrast to the fierceness of the baseball bat. "I love you."

The ambulance arrived and the attendants pushed through the crowd with the stretcher that would carry George to Englewood Hospital. The police would take Millie there.

Millie turned to Fenna, who now held the apron in her hands. "How did this happen? He didn't just fall, did he?"

The police had the same questions. They dispersed the crowd and moved the conversation into the Pedersen backyard. Fenna, Magnus, and Erik gave their accounts of the incident. Millie stood alongside listening, shaking her head, crying, and clenching and unclenching her fists.

Eventually the police escorted Millie to their squad car and slowly headed north, this time without sirens blaring or lights flashing. Millie thought about all the times she and George walked the half-block from Donegan's toward home, sometimes late at night, past this alley, without thinking about their safety. And now this, in broad daylight. What was happening to this neighborhood? This city?

Fenna threw the apron in the trash can by the alley and went into the house to clean up before taking the Halsted bus to Englewood Hospital.

Magnus finished fixing supper, although no one had much of an appetite. Erik and Kristen both noticed that Magnus forgot to pray before the meal. After a while Kristen asked, "Can we still play in the alley?"

The For Sale sign on the Clements' lawn was her only answer.

Four

In the quiet moments during worship at Grace Christian Reformed Church the next Sunday morning, Fenna's thoughts drifted to her visit with George Clement in the hospital the day before. She couldn't get George off her mind in the louder moments of worship, either. While the faithful meditated on the majestic Lord on high during the thunderous organ prelude, she thought about George Clement. As the congregation sang with their typically enthusiastic, slightly-off-key, near-harmony, Fenna's thoughts floated to not just George's physical discomfort but his mood. She couldn't focus as the congregation sang:

> Like a mighty army moves the Church of God;
> Brothers, we are treading where the saints have trod;
> We are not divided, all one body we,
> One in hope and doctrine, one in charity.
> Onward Christian soldiers, marching as to war,
> With the cross of Jesus going on before.

Nor did Fenna's mind still during the pastoral prayer. "O gracious and merciful God and Father," the Reverend Calvin Wolthuis prayed in his nasally, officious tone of deep holiness. "It behooves us to draw nigh unto Thee in the morning hour of this, the Sabbath day of Thy creation. We thank Thee that Thou hast established Thy covenant with believers and their seed. This Thou hast not only sealed by holy baptism, but Thou daily showest it by perfecting Thy praise out of the mouth of babes and sucklings, thus putting to shame the wise and prudent of this world."

The damage done to George is more than his cuts and bruises, Fenna thought. *I've never seen him so low.*

"We beseech Thee that Thou wilt increase Thy grace in them, in order that they may unceasingly grow in Christ, Thy Son, until they have reached complete maturity in all wisdom and righteousness."

Fenna's mind drifted to the scene in the alley and lingered there. *How is any of this going to be alright with George and Millie?*

"Give us grace to instruct them in Thy knowledge and fear, according to Thy commandment. May by their godliness the kingdom of Satan be destroyed and the kingdom of Jesus Christ in this and other congregations strengthened, unto the glory of Thy Holy Name and unto their eternal salvation, through Jesus Christ, Thy Son and our Lord, worthy of eternal praise and glory. Amen."

The Medemas were sitting behind the Pedersens. Eddie leaned forward as the prayer was concluding and tapped his finger on the top of the pew next to Erik. Three short. Three long. Three short. SOS. Just a few days earlier, they'd watched a show on TV where prisoners tapped Morse code messages to each other on the pipes in their jail cells. Erik snickered and Magnus elbowed him. Fenna didn't notice, she was still thinking of how George's comments in the hospital were so measured and reluctant and out of character for this man of mirth and good cheer. He seemed defeated.

"Fenna," George had said, "what's gonna happen to me and Millie?" He paused and looked out the hospital room window. "We didn't ask for this, you know."

"No one in his right mind would ask for this," Fenna said. There was a noise from the other side of the room—they weren't alone, there was another patient in the room, heavily sedated, who groaned on occasion.

Fenna and Millie both sat on the same side of George's bed. George looked smaller, wearing a hospital gown instead of his customary tee shirt, and there were dark circles under his eyes, which peered out below his bandaged scalp. Fenna had always thought of George as a feisty, larger-than-life character. Now he looked like a wounded, tired old man. This incident and injury had taken something out of him.

George lifted his shoulders off the bed and Millie gently helped situate his sheets and blanket. "All these years, nothin' ever happened—I mean nothin'. I never thought about nobody gettin' hurt, not me, not Millie, nobody. Sure, I had my scrapes back in the day. I admit to that. But I wanted those fights. Those I asked for, you know what I mean? This is different." He paused again, and looked around the room. "I knew who I was fightin' then. People like me. Fighting was just somethin' to do, ya know. Just somethin' we did in the neighborhood to make a name. But these kids—I mean, who are they? They didn't care one bit. What did they want from me? Money? You can't tell me this was about money. If they'd asked, I woulda given it to 'em right away. There was no need to beat on me like that."

"They did take your money though, right?" Fenna asked. "If it wasn't for money, what do you think this was about?"

The man in the other bed shifted.

"No way this was about money. They just wanted to scare the hell outta me. It was like they owned that alley and I shoulda known better than to be there. Hey, that's my alley—has been for years—it's your alley too. Where do they get off like they own it?"

Fenna said nothing and George closed his eyes. After a minute, his breathing calmed and he opened his eyes.

"Did they scare you enough to keep you out of the alley?" Fenna asked. "To keep you from coming through our yard?"

George let out a deep sigh. "I don't know, Fenna. I just don't know what to tell ya. They scared me. Don't know how much walking I'll be doin' anytime soon."

The doxology brought Fenna back to her church surroundings. The morning offering had been taken, this week for the support of seminarian Simon De Bolt, recently hired by Grace Christian Reformed Church for the work of neighborhood evangelism. The deacons marched to the front of the church with the offering plates and the Reverend Wolthuis gave the usual offertory prayer about God loving cheerful givers and imploring the Lord's blessing on De Bolt's work as he tended the Lord's vineyard and reaped the harvest, which was always plentiful while laborers were few.

Evangelism, to which the seminarian De Bolt was called, was a hard concept for a church that never knew what to do with outsiders. Enfolding a Norwegian Missouri Synod Lutheran like Magnus Pedersen had been a stretch for this collection of second and third generation Dutch immigrants, settled and satisfied with being surrounded by their own. Fenna was one of their own, and although Magnus was Protestant and not—heaven forbid—a papist Roman Catholic, Fenna's marriage to Magnus was a mixed marriage. According to the scriptures, Fenna and Magnus were unequally yoked. Not that Fenna and

Magnus cared. They'd met and married in their mid-thirties, and freely broke barriers.

Magnus's father had been a roofer. One day he had the misfortune of making a misstep while laying shingles and fell to the ground, crushing his right leg. He walked with a limp and cane the rest of his life.

His nurse in the Englewood Hospital was thin, blonde Fenna Boss, from Highland, Indiana, the former president of her nursing class. Magnus, with his mustache and bushy black hair, fell in love as Fenna tended to her patient.

Magnus was a steady visitor, certainly more regular than his siblings. Fenna had an inkling she knew why, which was confirmed when he asked her if she'd step into the hospital hallway. He had a question for her, a question, it turned out, that had nothing to do with his father's care. It was all about his care for her, and the beginning of a whirlwind romance.

They soon married, and outrageously hired a dance band for their wedding reception. Dancing was frowned on by the Christian Reformed Church—the joke was the church stood against premarital sex because it might lead to dancing. But Magnus and Fenna danced the night away at their celebration in a rented hall, in contrast to the common practice of celebrating in the church basement with ham buns and Jell-O salads served by the women of the congregation.

The focus of Simon De Bolt's work of "neighborhood evangelism," as assigned by the leadership of the church under the watchful eye of the Reverend Wolthuis, was to keep track of how close to the church Negroes were moving. De Bolt reported to the church council each month on which blocks to the east and the north were turning, had turned, and which blocks held the most For Sale signs. Rarely was De Bolt given the privilege of the pulpit to preach, but when he did, the young man showed promise. He wasn't nasally, looked the congregation in the eyes as he spoke, and preached for under forty minutes. His preaching was a pleasant surprise and predicted a bright future in ministry—but it was his record keeping on race that left the greatest impression.

Five

When Magnus Pedersen went to the church council meeting the next night, his fellow elders and deacons were talking about Friday's incident in the alley. With each retelling, the event took on new proportions. Now the attack had been perpetrated by four men in their early twenties, not three kids who were barely teenagers. Now one attacker had flashed a gun and the victim had been brutally pistol whipped and was near death. Now hundreds of dollars had been stolen and the Pedersens had risked their lives to save their neighbor. As so often happens when fear grabs hold of a group, truth was the victim. Magnus disappointed his fellow council members as he attempted to set the story straight. It was clear which version of events they preferred.

Council meetings were tests of mental and physical endurance, especially on warm, humid summer nights. They were held in a large windowless basement room, which was cool and damp as the meeting began. Before long, however, the body heat of twenty men sitting on hard wooden chairs, engulfed by the smoke of cigarettes and cigars (the Dutch smoked like chimneys), generated noticeable and predictable odors. The monthly meetings typically lasted three hours. Other congregants would speak to the men like they were in prison, asking: "How long are you in for?" and "When do you get out?" The Lord said his followers must be willing to pick up their cross, and he clearly had Christian Reformed Church council meetings in mind when he said it.

All former pastors of the church, living and dead, were permanent guests at each meeting, pictured in identical wooden frames on one wall of the room. Most were thickly bearded and there was not a smile among them—they looked as though their undergarments were as starched as their collars. Glaring into the room with doctrinal certainty, they dared anyone to stray from the true faith.

Typical topics on the agenda ranged from broken boilers to lapsed members to rumors about the Bible teacher at the local Christian school drifting toward liberalism. There never was a time when all were at peace in this hardwood Calvinist branch of the Protestant church tree. Yet there was something new on tonight's agenda: Rumors that Blacks from neighborhoods to the east—spurred on by the NAACP—were organizing to visit white churches in overwhelming numbers. What could the purpose be other than to disrupt worship and create a fuss?

This report came to the council's attention by way of seminarian Simon De Bolt, who was given the floor by the Reverend Wolthuis, keen on giving De Bolt a full internship experience. Many interns, like Daniel in the lion's den, were thrown into council meetings, but the Reverend Wolthuis was more careful and measured as he brought De Bolt along. It also gave the Reverend Wolthuis some distance from the information, in case someone might be inclined to shoot the messenger. De Bolt had picked up these reported rumors of disruption from pastors in areas where the racial mix was changing. His presentation was compelling, and to the defenders of the faith gathered like knights of the round table in the church basement, De Bolt's report was a call to action.

"Well, that's the last straw. Disrupting worship on the Lord's Day for some phony cause!" said Mel Lamsma, a real estate agent. "I heard the same thing from Gus Blonski from Regal Realty. We have two weeks to do something about this, so we better decide tonight."

"This is just the sort of thing being stirred up since that Martin Luther Junior Whatever spoke at that downtown Christian and Missionary Alliance Church last month," said Henk Koning, Pete's father and a first-generation immigrant from the Netherlands. "That man stirs trouble everywhere he goes. Comes to town, gets everyone boiled up, and leaves us with the mess."

Amid the nodding heads, the Reverend Wolthuis, who both relished the role of devil's advocate and yet found the mangling of King's name uncharitable, said, "Now, let's think this through. What if there's no truth to this rumor, no truth at all?" He looked around the room. "Why did you say we have two weeks, Mel?"

"Heard it at the realtor's association meeting the other day," Lamsma replied. "Even heard that they're hiring people from the west side to join them. They're looking to crowd all the white churches in this part of Englewood just to get a reaction."

"We need to be ready for the worst," said Carl Bensema, a deacon. The conventional view (far from official denominational polity) was that deacons were glorified ushers who handed out bulletins and collected the offering. Carl Bensema never would be elected to the position of elder, but the church always needed warm bodies as deacons. "We gotta hope for the best but plan for the worst," said Bensema, who could be counted on to be gloomy. "I say we lock the doors. If they try to break in, we call the cops."

That brought the discussion to a halt, and a restlessness settled over the room. Something didn't sit right about locking the church doors, although no one could find the words to express it.

The Reverend Wolthuis, sensing the discomfort, acted decisively by calling for a ten-minute break for coffee and pastries. It gave the men time to relieve themselves and form coalitions of opinion in the corners of the large church basement.

Magnus and his friend Meine Decker headed to a far corner. Like-minded on most matters, they usually looked for each other at breaks to debrief or let off steam. The Deckers had five tall and lanky boys and a basketball backboard in the alley at the opposite end of Green Street from the Pedersens.

"Really? Who are we kidding?" Meine began as he lit his second cigarette of the evening. Meine, a house painter, was soft-spoken but had a reputation for cutting to the chase in most conversations. "Who in their right mind would want to come to this church, Black or otherwise? You know better than anybody, Magnus, what it feels like to come here from the outside. You know how long it took for you to feel welcome here. How long before we stopped calling you Van Pedersen or Pedersensma, trying to make you Dutch with our stupid jokes? Why would anyone want to come here?"

"I'm thinking the same thing, Meine," Magnus said, lighting his own cigarette. "Not sure what the problem is other than the color of someone's skin. The Negroes I work with in the office are fine people, so I wouldn't mind if they came here. But I can't imagine why they'd want to." He scuffed a shoe on the floor. "You can't tell me that if we knew a flood of white folks were planning to visit, we wouldn't roll out the red carpet and sprinkle it with tulips. Anyone who innocently walked in here has no idea how inbred this church is, or how long it takes to really feel like you belong around here. I tell Fenna this church is just like a zoo. The only way we grow is by a birth or transfer from another zoo."

"Well, it's a certain kind of zoo," Meine said. "A zoo where you better only get together with your own kind. That's what we're teaching our kids."

Religious education was very serious business at the Grace Christian Reformed Church. Despite their reputation for saving a dollar, almost all the parents in the congregation spurned free public education and paid to send their children to the Christian school one block west of the church. Some parents paid tuition so their children would be insulated from the wider world. Others hoped that students would have their vision of the world—a vast mission field white unto harvest—expanded in the care of loving role models. Escape or engage? For the Dutch in Englewood, this tension played out over and over again in countless ways.

The capstone of religious education was making profession of faith, a rite of passage still on the horizon for twelve-year-old Erik Pedersen but one Meine and Wilma Decker's son Rich had successfully navigated a few months earlier. Profession of faith followed years of catechetical training every Wednesday immediately after school in the parish house next to the church. Catechism classes were taught by the Reverend Wolthuis, wearing his black preaching suit, vest, and wingtip shoes, which reinforced the gravity of the lessons. Over twenty years earlier, the Reverend Wolthuis had succeeded the legendary Willie Mensink as pastor. "Weeping Willie" was best known for how often his own sermons brought him to tears. The Reverend Wolthuis wasn't a weeper, but he knew his church's doctrinal standards as found in the Heidelberg Catechism, Belgic Confession, and Canons of the Synod of Dort the way many of the young people's fathers knew White Sox batting averages.

The only way for a kid to answer the Reverend Wolthuis's many questions in catechism class was through rote memorization, and for this reason the building was known as the "Perish House." Generations of young people had felt close to death as they struggled to answer the Reverend Wolthuis.

For the actual profession of faith, teenagers would appear before the elders for an interview, a conversation that routinely struck fear in the students. Already nervous, Rich Decker had encountered a question that threw him. It was a new question that went beyond the predictable "What is your only comfort in life and in death?" or "Why should Christians avoid worldly amusements such as those found in movie theatres?" Rich, who knew the exact price of a large buttered popcorn at the Capital Theater, was asked about interracial dating. He had never considered interracial dating, or any kind of dating for that matter. Rich wasn't the only one thrown by the question. Both Magnus and Meine were there, and the subject had never been discussed with the whole group of elders. How did a ban on interracial dating become church doctrine?

Meine was disturbed at this line of questioning about race and the assumptions that lay behind it. He wasn't all that certain about his own feelings, but knew his son shouldn't be pressured to believe one way or another. There was time for this soon enough.

Before the break ended, Meine and Magnus decided to make a motion to station volunteers at each door to welcome visitors, regardless of color. Meine offered the motion; Magnus seconded it. After several moments of palpable tension, the question was called. Meine and Magnus were the only ones to support it.

After more debate, discussion, deliberation, and fervent prayer for the leading of the Holy Spirit, Abram Versluis offered a new motion, one crafted in a different corner of the church basement by another, larger group during the break:

"I move that any coloreds who come here be ushered to seats in back rows reserved for them and then invited to meet with the council after the service to consider their motivation. Also, that our entry doors be locked five minutes after the service begins to prevent disturbances during worship. The congregation will be so informed of this policy decision." The motion carried with two dissenting votes.

Arnie Medema, Eddie's father, looked across the room at Meine and Magnus, and shrugged his shoulders, as if he were a helpless bystander at the scene of an accident. He had abstained from voting. Carl Bensema crossed his arms, stared at Magnus, and broke into a grin as a sign that he had played a decisive role in the decision. Magnus stared back.

Following a discussion concerning the recent trend of teenagers in the balcony disrupting the evening services, what to do with several unacceptable novels found in the church library, and whether a marimba is a musical instrument suitable for worship, the council meeting adjourned at 10:20 p.m. The Reverend Wolthuis walked slowly to his parsonage down the block, taking note of the homes of his parishioners along the way. He felt unsettled. He'd always valued unity and peace in the congregation, and that was slipping away. He was no social crusader, but the hatred some of his congregants had towards colored people was alarming. Maybe it was time to move on. Twenty-two years, he thought, is a reasonable tenure in one church.

His wife greeted him at the door, and the Reverend Wolthuis said nothing about the church meeting. He kissed her and said, "Good night, dear. I'm going to sit on the porch for some fresh air for a bit. Don't wait up any longer."

On the way to the porch, he went first to his study for his transistor radio, thinking that he might listen to police calls for a while, searching for evidence that the neighborhood was in peril and that he was leading the church in the right direction. His theological education equipped him for pastoring a church that valued doctrinal fidelity. It did little to equip him for the realities of a changing neighborhood, conflicts of conscience, or what leadership in this context looked like.

SIX

The doorbell rang just after the Pedersens finished dessert the next night (the kids' favorite, lime green Jell-O with sliced pears wobbling inside). Magnus was reading aloud the evening devotional, the story of Jesus casting a demon into a herd of swine, and Erik popped up to answer the door. His Uncle Mick was there, filling the door frame.

Mick O'Rourke, Erik's Irish Catholic uncle from the old neighborhood where Magnus grew up, was on duty. His police cruiser was parked at the curb. He held his Chicago police hat in his hands and asked if he could come in. Erik brought him into the kitchen and offered him his chair, which he filled, his thighs and large rear end smothering the seat. Uncle Mick was so huge Erik wondered how he could ever catch a criminal in a foot race, or even a brisk walk. Could Uncle Mick even keep up with the pigs in the story Magnus had just read? Erik wasn't sure. Uncle Mick also had a particular smell: day after day his Old Spice aftershave fought a losing battle against the smell of Lucky Strike cigarettes and Jim Beam bourbon.

Erik typically saw Uncle Mick at family gatherings, like those in Grandpa and Grandma Pedersen's small apartment off Garfield Boulevard on Sunday afternoons. And he always showed up for the raucous Pedersen Christmas parties: he would bring sacks of White Castle hamburgers while the rest of the family feasted at the potluck buffet. Beer flowed, other Pedersen uncles would join Magnus in a makeshift barber shop quartet for Christmas carols, and Uncle Swede would tell his bawdy joke about the Virgin Mary. Mick always seemed expressionless, sullen and sour, and sat by himself wherever he could find the roomiest chair. He'd married one of the Pedersen sisters, yet never fit in with the rest of the family. His sole contribution to conversation was "Hey Erik, bring me another sack," whenever he ran low on the small, greasy cheeseburgers with grilled onions and pickles on soft, steamed buns he brought with him. He'd then loudly make his annual joke: "They call 'em sliders, but it ain't clear if that's for how they go down or come out."

Tonight, Mick was all business, like Sergeant Joe Friday on *Dragnet,* only wider and without the suit, skinny necktie, and fedora.

"Those punks who jumped your neighbor are still out there," he said, addressing Magnus and Fenna. "Most likely doing their shit—pardon my French—somewhere else in the neighborhood. The report I read said that the whole family got a look at 'em, is that right?" Magnus and Fenna looked at each other. "So, who got the best look at 'em?" Magnus, Fenna, and Kristen impulsively looked in Erik's direction.

"Did anybody hear their voices, talk to them?" Uncle Mick was digging deeper.

"I did," Erik said. "Only one of them talked when he flashed a knife."

"You're our best witness," Mick said to Erik. "Listen," he said, turning towards Magnus and Fenna, "I want to take Erik for a ride and see if we can find 'em. He got the best look, right?" All heads nodded slowly and slightly. "Good. There's some chance he'll spot 'em on the street." He paused, sensing through the unease in the kitchen that this took them by surprise. "If that's okay with you."

Magnus hesitated, but this was police work, and the request was coming from a family member. "You'll keep my son safe?" Magnus said.

"Nothing to worry about," Mick said.

Erik thought it would be pretty cool riding in a police car through the neighborhood, even if it was with Uncle Mick.

"How long will you be gone?" asked Fenna.

"Maybe an hour. An hour at the most," Mick replied.

Magnus jumped in. "And what if you find them? If Erik recognizes them, then what?"

"Let's just say he'll do what's right by Mr. Clement. If he recognizes any of them, we'll cross that bridge then. Erik will be safe. I'll see to that."

Magnus and Fenna nodded their approval. Mick rose and the vinyl kitchen chair seemed to sigh in relief. Magnus said, "Be safe now, and do what's right."

Erik anxiously followed his uncle to the front door. What if he did see them? This would be a chance to set things right for Mr. Clement. He'd be a hero. He stepped out on the porch behind his uncle and saw the blue and white police car with the gumball red globe on top. He could see the sirens attached to the frame behind the back windows. "We Serve and Protect," was the new motto of the Chicago Police Department, detailed on the side of the car. Erik felt as though he'd just scored box seats for a White Sox vs. Yankees doubleheader. Who got to do this? Where were Pete, Frank, and Eddie? He wished they were here on the porch, watching his triumphal entry into a Chicago cop car. He glanced and saw that the Bensemas were already on their porch and looking at him.

Mick squeezed his body behind the steering wheel and motioned to Erik to sit in the front seat. Erik nodded towards the Bensemas, hoping they would figure out from his placement in the car that he was helping in an investigation. He was, after all, the Sherlock Holmes authority among the Green Street Boys. Uncle Mick pulled away from the curb without the sirens or the dome light operating.

When the Pedersens gathered on holidays, Mick was not in uniform. Now Erik soaked in every detail. His eyes were drawn first to the gun—cool gray steel in a worn leather holster. Erik wondered how often his uncle used it, if he'd ever shot anyone, and what it might feel like if he touched it or held it, but was afraid to ask. There was a Chicago flag with its four red stars on a white background sewn onto his uncle's right sleeve and a brass nameplate above Mick's right pocket that said "O'Rourke" with a number below it. The chatter and static of the police radio clicked on and off as they headed down Green Street, reminding Erik of the times he and his dad sat on the porch late at night and found police calls on their small transistor radio.

"Look," Mick said, "the plan is to head up Halsted to 71st Street, turn around and head south to 79th, and go up and down every alley and street east of Halsted this side of Hamilton Park. Just tell me when you see 'em. And you don't have to be a hundred percent positive. Just somebody that looks like 'em."

Erik was to finger—a police term he knew from *Dragnet*—one or more of the kids from the Clement incident. Then what? Would Uncle Mick arrest them, right there on the spot? He pictured those kids, handcuffed and angry, sitting in the back seat behind him.

And then what? Jail? Trials and testimony? Was he going to be a witness in court? And what did Uncle Mick mean about not being a hundred percent positive?

"Uncle Mick, you know it happened so fast," Erik said as the squad car slowly worked its way up Halsted. "I mean, I may be able to recognize the oldest guy, the one who showed me the knife. But the other two? I really didn't see them for that long. They were on top of Mr. Clement, rolling him over and looking through his pockets. And even the oldest guy ..." Erik paused. "I'm just not sure. I know he was bigger than me, but that's about it."

They turned around and headed south on Halsted. "Just keep looking, right to left. I'll go slow." They drove three blocks before Mick said, "Look, Erik, alls we're asking is your best guess. Kinda the process of elimination, understand? You know what they don't look like, right? Close is good enough."

"Close is good enough" did not feel right. They covered Halsted and then headed down an alley to the east at a slow crawl, brought to a temporary halt by a garbage truck emptying fifty-gallon drums. Then they stopped again for a back-door delivery to a store facing Halsted. Then another stop—there were kids playing baseball with a spongy rubber ball. Erik had learned to play baseball in his alley. You had to hit to center field—hitting to left or right meant the ball could be lost in a neighbor's yard or on the roof of some building. Erik looked at the game and wished he were out there. He saw a few kids he recognized from school and didn't know whether to wave or look away. Would those kids know he was on a police investigation or just think he was in trouble? He took his right arm away from the open window and slid down a bit in the passenger seat.

They went over to Emerald and the two blocks and alleys farther east before Mick pulled the squad car to the curb and said, "Look, Erik, you gotta think about what they did to your friend, right? You don't want them to get away with it, do you? Pay attention now, understand? It's not that hard. Remember, close is good enough. I'll take it from there."

As the squad car moved closer to Hamilton Park, the streets and alleyways became populated with more Black people—adults and kids—playing on sidewalks and sitting on front porches, in so many ways a mirror image of life west of Halsted. Erik was struck by the similarities so nearby and yet so far from his experience. Did they sit on their porches after supper and wait for the sun to go down on warm summer nights? As the squad car slowly advanced, they came upon a couple of girls jumping rope. When the girls saw the squad car, they dropped their rope and ran away. Nobody waved like they had in the alleys off Halsted. People either just stared as the squad car passed or rose from their porch and went inside.

"Okay, we're in the thick of coon town now," Mick said. "Let me know when you spot someone that looks like one of them."

"I don't know, Uncle Mick, I just don't know." Erik looked out the window straight ahead. "I mean, what are you asking me to do? I don't tell the whole truth about a lot of things—I know that—but this is something different. This is bigger. What those kids did was wrong, but this feels wrong too. I can't just get some random kid in trouble. And even if I saw the right guy and knew it for sure, what if he came after me later? They know where I live." He folded his skinny arms across his chest.

"I don't see them," Erik said. The car kept driving and he grew more and more uncomfortable. Time moved slowly as Uncle Mick's police car crawled through the alley. They drove on in silence until finally Erik said, "Maybe you should just bring me back home, Uncle Mick." A few awkward seconds later he added, "Please."

Mick stopped the car and turned to Erik, staring at him without saying a word. Erik looked away, but Mick took his right hand and firmly redirected Erik's head. "Hey, look at me, Erik. Don't screw this up." Erik could smell Mick's sour breath and clearly see his crooked yellow teeth. "This is your chance to be a hero. Are you gonna disappoint your friend George? Think about what he looked like suckin' dirt and blood in the alley. What kind of friend are you? I didn't take you for a coward."

"Maybe. Maybe I am," Erik said. He leaned back but was unable to escape Mick's strong grip. "Just bring me home, Uncle Mick. Just bring me home. Unless, maybe you want to stop at White Castle first," Erik said, hoping to lighten the moment. Mick pushed Erik away and started the car. He didn't say a word all the way to Erik's house on Green Street. There were still a few people out on their porches, and Erik saw Old Man Finnegan glaring at him as the police car approached.

At the curb, Mick said, "Look, Erik, I hope someday you get some balls 'cause you ain't got 'em now." As Erik slowly opened the car door and gave his uncle one last look, Mick sneered. "You have a good night now. Get your pink jammies on and crawl in bed with your teddy bear."

Erik walked slowly up the short sidewalk with his hands in his pockets and avoided looking at his parents or sister, who were out on the porch. He walked past them and went into his room, where he slumped onto his bed and buried his head in his pillow. He felt like crying but didn't. Instead, he replayed the ride over and over, thinking about what Uncle Mick asked him to do and how it didn't feel right. He couldn't stop thinking about the way the Black people they passed stared at the police car, how things came to a halt as they drove by, and how he'd seen some parents gathering their kids into their arms when they saw the words "We Serve and Protect."

Seven

"C'mon. Spill it," Pete Koning said as he walked onto the Pedersens' porch. The Green Street Boys were gathering the next morning, but Frank and Eddie weren't even on the porch yet. Pete sat on the ledge he always claimed and Erik was on the top step. Frank and Eddie were walking up now, almost within earshot, and Erik waited to be sure they could hear his response.

"It was kind of a thrill and not a thrill, know what I mean?" Erik said, picking up his baseball glove that had sat out on the porch for a couple of days. He fiddled with his glove and then said, "Don't know that I'll ever forget it. Not sure I *should* forget it."

Frank and Eddie settled onto the porch. "Was it scary?" Frank asked. "Were you afraid?"

"Ever met my Uncle Mick?" Erik said. "He's the scariest guy I know. Biggest, too. Plus, he has really bad breath. He didn't smile at all when we were in the car. He's always sort of angry." He looked into his glove. "Yeah, I was pretty scared. At first, I thought it was great, being in a cop car and all, but after a while, I couldn't wait to get home."

It was a perfect summer day, and any other summer the Green Street Boys would have gotten off the porch and into the neighborhood doing something. The summer of 1962 was when all that changed. There had been a time when the Green Street Boys would jump on their bikes and ride to places like the Museum of Science and Industry or even Midway Airport and their parents wouldn't have minded. They even invented their own detective agency inspired by the adventures of Sherlock Holmes, following customers leaving National Tea on foot, writing detailed descriptions of their "suspects" in spiral notebooks. This sleuthing took them across the dividing line of Halsted into an integrated neighborhood. Now, their parents put a halt to all these adventures. The Green Street Boys kept hearing the word "safety" from their parents. In the name of safety, boundaries had been imposed from dangers none of the boys were sure existed.

They missed Midway the most. At the airport they would lie on their backs on the scruffy grass at the corner of 63rd and Cicero and watch the planes come in for a landing right above their heads. The powerful thrust of wind generated would whip the streamers on their bikes around and they'd yell at each other but not be able to hear because of the noise. The new jet airliners landed at O'Hare, which was too far to pedal to, so they settled for the smaller, louder prop planes at Midway. Every plane looked as though it were about to crash right on top of them as it glided over the rooftops of the neighborhood to the southeast. Frank always claimed he'd scouted out a safe spot he could get to if a plane crashed, the others just figured they'd take their chances.

The trip to the museum was a bit shorter and on the way they'd argue about what they would do once they arrived at the huge grey remnant of the World's Columbian Exposition. Some argued for descending to the bowels of the Earth to the coal mine, with its creaky, snail-paced, frightening elevator creeping into the darkness below. Others preferred the claustrophobic U505 German submarine, captured during World War II when a Nazi captain failed to make a left turn at Morocco.

"Why would we want to go to the coal mine?" Frank would inevitably say. "It's just a slow ride to the stinking basement, that's all. Same floor as the cafeteria. The whole thing is fake. And the elevator guy always mumbles. You can't understand what he's saying."

"Exactly," Pete would say, for once agreeing with Frank about something. "Plus, the guy running the elevator is supposed to be a miner except he's a hundred and six years old so who puts a guy like that in a mine, and anyway the soot on his face looks like shoe polish. I want to go to the submarine. My dad was in the war in Holland, and he says it's the real deal."

Airplanes, submarines, coal mines, long distance bike trips, that was the stuff of summer. But now, life up and down Green Street and throughout the neighborhood west of Halsted was noticeably different. Now Erik was riding in police cars.

"Wait, wait. Start over," Pete said. "I saw you but I don't know why were you in the cop car to begin with."

Erik pulled one of the leather laces on his baseball glove tight. "My uncle wanted me to ride with him into the Black neighborhood and see if I could pick out the guys who beat up Mr. Clement."

"You kiddin' me?" Frank said. "Get out! I'd die to do that!"

"Bullcrap, Frank!" Eddie said. "You'd wet your pants as soon as the cop car door slammed."

Frank was undeterred. "Well, did you find the guys? How long was the ride? Did he let you hold his gun?"

"One thing at a time," Erik said. "It didn't turn out the way I thought it would. I thought it was kinda cool when I got in his car, right there in the front seat and all. His gun was right next to me." Erik opened and closed his glove a few times. "But he wanted me to pick anyone off the street and say he did it. Whether he did it or not, anybody I picked was the one who attacked Mr. Clement. Just anybody!"

"Well, did you nail anyone?" Frank said.

There was a pause and then Eddie said, "Of course he didn't, ignoramus! That's the whole point. What do you think you would have done?"

Eddie was looking at Frank, but it was Pete who answered. "Honestly?" he said. "I might have picked someone off the street. I'm guessing that if he wasn't the one, he probably knew who did it. And if he did know who did it, he'd tell the cops who did it so he'd go free. So, yeah, I get what your uncle was doing. Like on *The Untouchables*. You know. Pick someone up, bring him into the station, shine a bright light on the guy in a hot room, make him sweat, and before you know it, he's saving his skin. He'd name somebody to get outta there. No doubt."

"Yeah," Frank said. "I'd nail somebody."

"But what if he didn't do it?" Erik said, looking at Pete and then Frank. "And what if he couldn't name anybody because he really, truly didn't know who did it?" Erik looked out across the street. "You think all Black kids know every other Black kid?" Erik noticed he was squeezing his fingers inside his glove and relaxed.

"I don't know," Pete said. "Maybe not. But I get what your uncle was doing. Probably what you need to do sometimes to get the job done." They paused as a moving truck rattled past down the street.

"You know that dime store that was held up last week, the one on 79th?" Eddie said. "How about I just call Erik's Uncle Mick and tell him I think you did it?"

"Yeah, I'm good with that!" Frank said, "Don't worry, Pete, I'll visit you in jail!"

"Don't be stupid!" Pete said, looking around at the others. "Think about it. Picking one of them off the street makes sense. They all look alike anyway, right?"

"Where did you get that?" Eddie said.

"That's what my dad says, and he works with a lot of them, so he should know."

"Minnie Miñoso looks like Martin Luther King," Erik said, "who looks like Sidney Poitier? You're so full of crap! And so is your dad." Erik threw his glove at Pete, who brushed it aside.

"What did you say?" Pete stood up. "Say what about my dad?"

Erik and the others didn't stand up.

Pete wouldn't let it go. "OK, I suppose you say that because you know so many coloreds. But who do you really know? Name one. Not from TV, or sports, or movies, nothing like that. I mean up close and personal. How many do you know for real?"

Not one of them could name a Black kid or adult they actually knew.

After a long pause, Pete spoke again. "Then in my book you don't know what you're talking about. And don't talk about my dad unless I ask you to." Pete sat back down and picked up Erik's glove.

Erik took stock in the silence around him. Pete was right. He didn't know a single Black person. Never talked with one. Never played ball with one. Never laughed or argued with one. The closest contact for Erik was when he went with his dad, Meine Decker, and Meine's sons to the Helping Hand Mission on Madison, where they would lead a hymn, play musical instruments, and deliver their testimony. The people there had to listen to them to get a free dinner in the basement of the mission—only those who endured the service were permitted downstairs for the meal and a night's rest. The audience was always a mix of white and Black men.

"Look," Erik said. "I'm sorry I said what I did about your dad. I shouldn't have said that. And you're right, I don't even know one colored person. But still, there's no way they all look alike."

"So, when all's said and done," Frank said, "You're still full of crap!" Erik and Eddie both laughed and eventually Pete shook his head and gave Erik a light tap on the shoulder with Erik's baseball glove.

EIGHT

It only took a few weeks after the For Sale sign appeared on the Clements' lawn for the word "SOLD" to be added atop it. Before that happened, Florence Bensema had seen a young Black couple arrive to tour the Clement house with the realtor, and that evening Carl Bensema confronted his neighbor, accusing him of selling out the neighborhood.

"Look," George Clement said as he stepped onto his porch to talk to his neighbor, "the only color I care about is green. As long as their money is green, I don't care about any other color. Green looks good to me."

"You can't do this," Carl said.

"You'll understand when your day comes," George said. "Who do you think you'll sell to?"

Carl poked his finger at George's chest. "Well, screw you, and good riddance." He turned and stomped up the steps of his house two at a time, and tried to slam the screen door for added effect, but the door's gentle closing mechanism stymied him. George Clement watched, shook his head, and went back inside his house.

The evening the word SOLD appeared on the Clements' For Sale sign, the Pedersens crossed the street and rapped on the Clements' door. Millie appeared, wiping her hands on her apron.

"Welcome friends, welcome," she said. "Come on inside. Guess you noticed the sign?"

"Well, yes, we did," Fenna said, as they stepped into the Clements' foyer. "That didn't take too long, did it?"

"No, not at all. Kind of surprising," Millie said. "It's all happening so quickly. I can hardly catch my breath, there's so much to do."

George heard the voices and joined them. "Hello, hello!" he said, as he put his huge hand on Erik's head and mussed his hair. "Come on in, why don't ya? Did Millie tell you we've found a place?" He didn't wait for an answer. "In Indiana, just over the border. Munster, just off Ridge Road. It's smaller than this, a ranch, so no stairs to climb. And looks to be a place where we won't have to worry about being safe and all." As George talked, the conversation moved into the living room, which was strewn with newspapers for wrapping belongings. Filled and labeled boxes were stacked on the dining room table.

"It ain't easy starting over in a smaller place," Millie said, "but it's high time we get rid of some stuff. All these years it just piles up, you know?

"Isn't it amazing how much stuff we accumulate?" Fenna said as she moved some newspapers aside so she could sit on the Clements' couch.

"And so much of it junk," Millie said. "George is having a hard time parting with his collection of beer mugs in the garage. You wouldn't believe it! Must be twelve shelves full. I pitch 'em when he's not looking." She winked at Fenna and laughed.

"Well this is a big step for you two. How do you feel?" Fenna asked.

"Speaking of beer," George said as he stood, "can I pour you one, Magnus?"

"I'm fine," Magnus said from the couch next to Fenna, holding up his hand. "Just had supper." Erik and Kristen couldn't find chairs, so they sat on the floor near their parents. Erik looked intently at George's head, looking for signs of where the bat had hit him.

"Sit down, George," Millie said. "Fenna asked me a question and I intend to answer it." She turned and faced Fenna. "You don't make a move like this without second guessing yourself. Lived here almost our whole married lives. It's been a good place to live. And we've enjoyed having you as our neighbors. Can't thank you enough for being there through the mess in the alley and George's recovery. Can't thank you enough for all you've done."

"And we'll miss you kids too," George said, looking at Erik and then Kristen. "But you can always come visit us."

"We'd like that," Erik said.

"There's something we need to tell your folks," George said. "Might as well tell all of you, you'll find out soon enough. We sold the house to coloreds." George shook his head slightly.

"They're a young couple," Millie said. "Don't think they have kids. Last name of Jackson. He's a minister and she's a teacher."

Magnus and Fenna looked at each other without saying a word.

By the end of that week the Clements officially became Hoosiers. Two days later, the Jacksons moved in, the first Black presence on that section of Green Street.

Willowby and Sheila Jackson moved into their new small white frame house in the middle of the day, a risk given the history of racial violence in south and west Chicago. Willowby felt strongly that this step up from their crowded apartment in Woodlawn was a way to preach what was important to them. He was inspired that many civil rights leaders were preachers like himself, and believed that the scriptures called him not just to preach the gospel but live the gospel. "Live life faithfully for others to see" was his credo, and Sheila felt the same way.

They had met while she was an undergraduate at the University of Chicago and he was earning a doctor of divinity degree from the seminary there. The two were among the few Blacks at this northern gothic fortress, and met sitting next to each other on the floor of the administration building protesting discriminatory housing practices in the Woodlawn neighborhood adjoining campus. They soon realized each other came from the deep South and shared similar views on many things. Now married, they had decided to make Chicago their home, fully aware of the danger inherent in the divided and often violent city.

Willowby Jackson wanted to be different. Instead of staying in Mississippi, where sincere but uneducated Black pastors were as plentiful as the hand-held fans moving the air on any given summer Sunday, he came north to Chicago for divinity school and to learn how to be a pastor. After working in a small West Side church while he was in seminary, he'd taken a call to the Greater Freedom Methodist Church.

Church politics and Chicago politics often moved in contentious dances around who held power in a neighborhood, and serving a church in an area of racial change like Englewood demanded skill, wisdom, and a willingness to serve with boldness.

Sheila was a teacher at Lindblom Technical High School in west Englewood. There'd been tremendous change in the makeup of the student body in recent years, and now most students were Black. Lindblom was one of the largest high schools in the city. As the population shifted, so did the resources given to schools, and her classroom was typical of those in Black neighborhoods: overcrowded, under-resourced, and in need of repair. She taught English and served as the adviser to the Chess Club. Her colleagues were mostly old white men, crusty veteran teachers who still clung to the belief that Lindblom was a school for the children of European immigrants.

"Never seen so many teachers looking forward to retirement," Sheila said to Willowby after her first full week at Lindblom. They were just settling down to dinner and she spooned out some mashed potatoes. "Most of them talk like they don't care anymore. They don't make a secret of it." Sheila found teaching thrilling, her students engaging, but collegiality as rare as snow on summer pavement.

Unlike the small storefront churches along busy streets in Englewood, Greater Freedom Methodist Church was an edifice of substance, a solid brick and stained-glass corner church. For decades, the building had been the site of the Ebenezer Christian Reformed Church of Englewood until its members left for the suburbs. Now there was an attractive lighted sign out front inviting the neighborhood to attend worship under the leadership of the Reverend Doctor Willowby Jackson. He carried credentials with weight and substance, but he also knew that fancy signage, bricks, and stained-glass windows meant nothing without a strong voice for justice in the lives of his congregation.

There were both morning and evening services on Sundays at Grace Christian Reformed Church and it was customary for Magnus and Fenna to gather with friends after the evening worship service. The Sunday night after the Jacksons moved in, the Pedersens hosted coffee at their home. They'd invited their friends Meine and Wilma Decker, Arnie and Evelyn Medema, and the seminary intern Simon De Bolt. They'd hosted the Reverend and Mrs. Wolthuis on plenty of occasions, and were hoping Simon De Bolt might bring a little more excitement to their gathering. Apart from school events and church socials, Sunday night coffee was the gathering place for the latest news of neighborhood changes, gossip, rumors, and sophisticated one-upmanship, depending on the storyteller.

"Coffee" also gave the women the chance to showcase their baking skills, with desserts prepared without consulting the *Betty Crocker Cookbook* or the limited edition, spiral-bound collection of recipes entitled *Better than Betty: The Goodness of Grace Cookbook* (a controversially prideful title), that was sold as a fundraiser for missionaries serving in a foreign field. Making a dessert from a recipe in a book was looked down on as a form of culinary plagiarism and could never be served to guests. The most exotic desserts were usually topped with the extravagance of real whipped cream, and if one of the husbands offered a compliment, his wife was bound by an unwritten code to ask for the recipe. Erik and Kristen loved the occasional Sunday nights when their parents were the entertainers, the living room furniture fully occupied, the noise of conversation filling the night as clouds of cigarette smoke floated near the ceiling. The Pedersen children fought to stay awake in their bedrooms so they could listen to the adult conversation.

Not unusually, on this night the women were in the kitchen with Fenna while the men grabbed their desserts and coffee and settled in the living room.

"Who's your new neighbor?" Meine Decker asked.

"I don't really know," Magnus said. "George Clement told me the name and I can't say I remember."

"It's Jackson," Simon De Bolt said.

"Yes, that's right. Jackson," Magnus said. "But how in the world do you know that?"

"He's a minister," De Bolt said.

"That's right," Magnus said. "George said that. But how do you know? Do you guys all keep track of each other?" Magnus got up from the couch to bring the coffee pot around again.

"He's colored," De Bolt said.

"Is he?" Meine Decker said. "Oh me. Right next door to Carl Bensema."

"I knew he was colored but I didn't know he was a minister," Arnie Medema said.

"Methodist," De Bolt said.

"Is he?" Meine said as he swallowed a bit of pineapple upside down cake. "So Magnus, is it a bigger problem that he's colored or that he's a Methodist?"

All the men except De Bolt laughed. "What's so funny?" Fenna asked, as she led Wilma Decker and Evelyn Medema out from the kitchen.

"Just talking about your new neighbors," Meine said. "Young Simon here knows everything about them. Say, De Bolt, what's his hat size?"

More laughter followed, and then the phone rang in the kitchen. Fenna excused herself and went to answer it. The tone of her voice stopped the conversation in the living room. "Oh no! No, that's awful! Are you sure?" Fenna said. Erik and Kristen heard their mother and both got out of bed and inched their doors open to hear better. "What will happen to that family now? Four kids, right? What will they do?"

Fenna paused and gathered her thoughts before slowly returning to the living room, where she was met with silence and stares. "It's Fred DeVries," she said. Fred DeVries was a milkman and member of Grace Christian Reformed Church. He'd been robbed and shot the day before on his milk delivery run. The news had spread quickly through the congregation and neighborhood, and prayers for his recovery had been offered just an hour earlier at the evening service. "He's dead."

There was a stunned silence in the living room.

This news sent Kristen back to bed, but Erik stayed up sitting by his door, listening to the angry, confused, adult conversation that followed. Mr. DeVries was their milkman. Erik went to school with his children. Who would shoot a milkman? He could hear Simon De Bolt insisting it must have been Negroes while Meine and his dad argued against jumping to conclusions. Erik thought of the knife-wielding attackers of George Clement and knew life in Englewood had again just taken a sudden and sharp turn.

It would be years before he could articulate what he felt that night: fear, invasive and insidious, like a caustic unwelcome guest who would never leave. This whole summer felt like quicksand with no one coming to the rescue.

Nine

Fred DeVries had been the consummate milkman. Like those who delivered the mail, he was never kept from his appointed rounds by rain, sleet, snow, or ice. Dressed in his starched white pants and shirt, black bowtie, and white hat with the black "Bowman Dairy" letters stenciled above the brim, Fred often whistled a tune or hummed a hymn as he left his truck and crossed the sidewalk loaded with milk bottles in a wire carrier. Sometimes he'd take the steps to a porch two at a time, depending on his schedule and the number of conversations he'd had with customers along the way. The more they talked, the more he'd have to hustle. And Fred was a talker. Yet he was an even better listener, which endeared him to his customers. As did his black bowtie and his black suspenders.

He had spoken often to friends with concern about his future. Supermarkets were springing up in neighborhoods, exemplified by National Tea right there on Halsted. He could see that the days of delivering milk to front porches, placing the fresh bottles in the insulated box on the front stoop, and taking the empties along with new order notes and payments with him back to the truck were numbered. He would miss the good hard work and the customers he served, both white and Black as the neighborhood changed. Yet he never shared his uncertainty about the future with his wife Eleanor. He didn't want to worry her.

Fred felt comfortable in the new Black sections of Englewood. He was a member of the Grace Christian Reformed Church and he'd heard all the negative talk at church. But getting to know his new customers opened his mind and heart. He'd concluded that Black people were just that, people, and the most important thing about them wasn't the color of their skin but that they needed milk delivered like anybody else. He wished that more of his old friends would have the opportunity to meet the people on his route. When he tried to talk about his customers on the east side of Halsted, few of his friends wanted to hear about it.

From their new front porch, the Jacksons looked east across Green Street, directly at the Pedersen bungalow. They'd waved and smiled at each other, but had not met. The waves and smiles were more than they got from other new neighbors, yet Willowby still wanted more. He knew he probably was dreaming, but he wanted to be known and accepted. At least there had been no incidents. There were no white mobs protesting their breach of boundaries, no eggs thrown at the house, no bricks through the front windows.

Willowby thought since he was the new person on the street, the established residents should break the ice. But that wasn't happening. He was unsure of the protocol in white neighborhoods, and so had waved and smiled at the Pedersens but not crossed the street to talk to them. There were plenty of opportunities; most nights he saw them sitting on their porch after supper. A couple of evenings after the Pedersens learned of the death of Fred DeVries, Willowby decided not to wait any longer.

He stepped out on his porch, took his hands from his pockets, paused to stretch, waved at the man sitting alone on his porch across the street from him, and walked down the stairs of his new home. As he crossed the street, there were parked cars on both sides of the street to navigate through, and then he walked right up to the man sitting alone and reached out and took his hand.

"Greetings neighbor! I'm Willowby Jackson. I thought it was high time that we met."

The white man in front of Willowby stood as they shook hands and appeared to be blushing. Then the man looked to his right and left and said, "I'm Magnus Pedersen. Nice of you to come over. I live here with my wife and our kids, Erik and Kristen." He looked to his right and left again. "My wife Fenna, she might step out here any moment." He turned toward the house and in a loud voice said, "Fenna."

"Well, I look forward to meeting them," Willowby said. "And for you to meet my wife, Sheila. We haven't had the chance yet to meet too many folks since we moved in. Seems we keep noticing each other across the street, so I thought I'd start with you."

Magnus looked around again. "Fenna," he said into the house again. Magnus then looked intently at something over Willowby's shoulder, and Willowby asked, "Should I turn around or are you going to tell me what's over my shoulder?"

"It's not what, it's who," Magnus said. "I just noticed the Bensemas staring at us. Carl and Florence."

"Should I turn around and wave at them?" Willowby said, smiling.

"I don't recommend it," Magnus said.

Just then the screen door opened and Fenna, untying her apron, said, "Well, look who's here!"

"Yes," Willowby said. "In the flesh."

"I'm Fenna."

Willowby looked confused.

"I know it's an odd name. It's Dutch. We're Dutch. Or at least I'm Dutch. Magnus isn't. But you already guessed that. I never would have named myself Fenna, sounds kinda strange, doesn't it? Like an herb or spice or something."

Willowby smiled and said, "I like it, it's a good rich name. How can you forget a 'Fenna'? Or a Magnus? Anyway, my name is Willowby and there's a story behind that. My sharecropper grandparents down South worked a plantation loaded with weeping willows along the riverbank. Parents named me to keep the grandparents' memory alive, you see. They felt names should tell stories. My wife is Sheila. No story there far as I know. She teaches at Lindblom Tech. English grammar and literature. I'm the pastor of Greater Freedom Methodist Church over near Hamilton Park. Maybe you've heard of it?"

Both Magnus and Fenna looked at their feet.

"Used to be Ebenezer Christian Reformed Church," Willowby said.

"Oh sure, we know that," Magnus said.

Willowby could see the Pedersen kids inside, watching them but staying away from the door. "We'd like to have you over to our porch some night," Willowby said. "Just wanted to stop over and say hello for starters. It's been good to meet you. You have a good night."

As he was turning to leave, Fenna said, "We'd like that, Reverend Jackson—Willowby. We'll make work of that. And say hello to Sheila for us." Willowby smiled, nodded, and made his way back across the street, feeling as though he'd just crossed the Grand Canyon on a tight rope. He could still hear their voices behind him, saying, "Why didn't you ask him to sit down?" and "What's a sharecropper?"

When he returned home, Willowby sat on the couch in front of the bay window in his new living room, peeking out at the Pedersens, still on their porch.

"What are you up to now?" Sheila asked, seeing him scrunched down on the living room sofa. "What's happening out there?" Without turning to acknowledge her, Willowby waved her over to join him and patted the couch for her to take a seat.

Sheila shook her head no and remained standing. "I'm fine right here. I don't need to spy on anyone. Besides, I've got papers to grade."

Looking up at her, Willowby said, "I just crossed through the Red Sea on dry land. Went across the street to meet our neighbors. I thought I'd see if we could break through with some folks on this block, and the ones across the street are the only ones who even wave. We could do with some friends on this street. Lord knows we'd wait forever for the man next door to do anything. Sits on his porch like he's Buddha, smoking his cigar and reading the paper. I could be on fire and he wouldn't budge."

"Hold on just a minute," Sheila said. "Walking across the street to say hello to white folks we don't know is going to help us how? How do you figure that's what I need, what we need? Making friends is the least of my worries. We have plenty of friends. You know that, right?"

"Sheila, honey," Willowby said, standing to face her. "Look, how can it hurt? They seem like nice folk. The Pedersens, Magnus and Fenna, that's their names. Can't remember the names of the kids. I told them just a bit about us. Not too much. Said we'd have them over some night for a chat on the porch, and they seemed to like that. Said they would. It's a start at something."

Sheila had her red grading pencil in her hands and realized she'd been absentmindedly bending it. She stopped before it snapped. "And that's going to solve what exactly?" Sheila said. "Will that make us safer? Talking with them, will that help me sleep at night, Willowby? I get the glares and stares all day at school from my colleagues, and I come home to wonder if tonight is the night we'll hear glass shatter or smell smoke and need to run out of here. And you want to have a sweet little chat with folks across the street, is that right?"

"I said we'd have them over, just a porch chat, doesn't have to be long. You can do that, can't you?"

"This isn't the University of Chicago, Willowby. We're not surrounded by like-minded folk. We're not on the same team on this block. Who knows what these new friends of yours have on their hearts because of us moving in here? It's not like it was back in the South where at least white people admitted they hated us. Up here they still hate us, but they're polite about it."

Willowby looked at her. Was this a real fight? He wasn't sure. "I know we're not in Mississippi," he said. "We're here now. We've got to make the best of all this, you and me, together. It's not a big risk to have them over. We'll see what's on their hearts. It won't be but an itty-bitty sit on our porch." Willowby slipped his arms through hers and around her back and gave two soft kisses on her graceful neck.

Sheila pulled away and waved the pencil at him. "Nice try, Reverend."

As he turned from Sheila back to the view from the living room he saw Magnus and Fenna moving across the street in their direction, waving at the Bensemas, and walking up their stairs. As the doorbell rang, Sheila spun around and tilted her head at Willowby, and said, "Now look what you've done."

Ten

Willowby went to the door and said, "Well, that didn't take long, did it?" He opened the door and extended his hand and welcomed Magnus and Fenna with a laugh, not daring to look at Sheila.

"Surprise, right?" Fenna said. "Like they say, 'Never put off today what you could put off until tomorrow.'"

Willowby looked puzzled, but smiled.

"We talked about your invitation and thought that there was no time like the present," Magnus said. "You kind of surprised me earlier tonight and I didn't want you to misunderstand. That we don't like you. I mean that we do like you. I mean we don't know you and we want to get to know you."

"Sure," Willowby said. "You haven't met Sheila yet. I apologize."

"How does lemonade sound?" Sheila said, joining them in the doorway. "I just made a pitcher full. Willowby, grab some chairs and we'll sit on the front stoop."

Willowby brought out chairs for Magnus and Fenna, and he and Sheila poured everyone a lemonade and then sat on the stairs alongside them. Once they were settled on the porch,

Sheila asked, "How long have you lived here on Green Street? We'd love to hear your story."

Magnus and Fenna both started talking at once, but Magnus gradually ceded the floor to Fenna, who began with their marriage, having children, living in a small apartment east of Halsted, and then achieving the dream of a bungalow, with a basement and an attic and their very own backyard.

"So, even before you moved across the street you were well established in Englewood, is that right?" Willowby asked.

Magnus said, "We have a lot of connections to this neighborhood. Fenna worked at Englewood Hospital on 55th as a nurse before the children came. Our church is here and so is the school our children attend. Maybe you've driven past them: Grace Christian Reformed on Peoria and Englewood Christian School on Sangamon? Within walking distance. And I went to high school at Lindblom."

"Seems like you have everything you need right here," Sheila said. "That must be nice."

"Yes, it is," Fenna said. "That's true for any number of families up and down this block." There was a pause and Fenna looked at her lemonade. "Good lemonade," she said as she wiped the condensation off her glass, causing Sheila to smile.

Another moment passed and then Willowby said, "So, tell us about the previous owners of this house. We met them but know little about them. We had a lawyer take care of the sale details."

Magnus and Fenna looked at each other. "Say, it's getting dark," Magnus said, "and our kids will be coming home when the streetlights come on. While I tell you about George and Millie, help us keep an eye open for them."

"Remind me of the names of your children," Willowby said. As Fenna and Magnus both said, "Erik and Kristen," Sheila rose and asked if anyone wanted a lemonade refill. When she returned, Magnus and Fenna took turns offering detail after detail about George and Millie Clement, edited to avoid the attack in the alley. The words "salt of the earth" came up often, and "grandparents to every kid around here." They focused on Millie's cookies and George's genial nature with everyone in the neighborhood and his daily habit of walking over to Donegan's through their alley and then heading to National Tea for a newspaper before he came home.

"Well," Willowby said, "I'd like to be friendly to the kids in the neighborhood but I can't say I am going to be in a bar every afternoon."

"You better not be," Sheila said, and Magnus and Fenna laughed.

"Are those your kids?" Willowby asked, seeing Erik and Kristen walking toward home.

Fenna stood and waved them over, and they ambled across the street to join them.

Erik spoke before they'd even reached the stairs: "I'm guessing you've already heard about us. We get around." Erik laughed at his own joke and his parents smiled. "We used to sit on this porch a lot," Erik said. "Mr. Clement was a funny old guy. Loved to tell jokes and stories about when he worked for the railroad."

"Do you remember any of his jokes?" Willowby asked.

"Not really," Erik said, "but if I did, I'd get in trouble with my mom if I told you one." That got a laugh from the adults, and Erik spoke again. "So, did my parents tell you about his beating? I saw it happen."

Fenna raised a hand to her bowed forehead and rubbed it. Willowby and Sheila both looked at Magnus.

"Yes, it was at the beginning of summer," Magnus said reluctantly. He described coming home to find George on the ground in the alley with three boys standing over him.

"How old were these boys?" Willowby asked.

"I don't know," Magnus said. "They were just kids. Street kids."

"Younger than Erik?"

"Oh, I wouldn't say that."

"One of them pulled a knife on me," Erik said. "A switchblade. Later, I got to ride in a cop car. My Uncle Mick's a cop, and he drove me around Hamilton Park looking for them, but I didn't see them."

"My church is by Hamilton Park," Willowby said.

A stillness settled over the conversation, a discomfort that matched the discomfort of the humid summer night at sunset.

Willowby stood and said, "I just want to stretch my legs. He walked down the steps and turned to face the Pedersens and Sheila on the porch. "So, you say this was what—six or eight weeks ago? And the police haven't found the attackers yet, I assume."

"As far as we know," Magnus said. "We've not read anything in the papers or heard anything new from my brother-in-law."

"I'm very sorry about this," Willowby said. "I can't imagine how awful this must have been for the Clements. And scary for you all to get in the middle of it. And now the killing of the neighborhood milkman. Almost too much to handle, right?"

"You know about Fred DeVries?" Fenna asked.

"He was the milkman for many in our church," Sheila said. "And dearly loved. From what we've heard a good man—like Mr. Clement—always with a smile and a word to brighten someone's day. Willowby and I have been praying for his family since we heard."

"So have we," Fenna said.

"I go to school with one of his daughters. Jean," Kristen said.

"And I know their son Gary," Erik said.

"We attend the same church," Magnus said, "and Fred's been a milkman for many years. A lot of people are going to miss him."

"Well, we want you to know that we and our church pray for his family," Willowby said. "Our prayer is that justice will win out. Whoever did this should be brought to trial."

The lemonade glasses were empty and Magnus looked at his watch. "We've got to get these kids home and in bed," he said, as he and Fenna stood. "Thanks for a nice evening."

Willowby whispered to Sheila as they watched the Pedersens walk across the street. "Did you hear the name of the church they attend? Same as the group we bought our building from."

"So what?" Sheila said.

"Doesn't that give you pause?"

"Why should it?"

"They're Dutch Reformed, cousins of those hard-headed folks in South Africa, the Afrikaaners, who are making life so difficult for our people there."

"Willowby Jackson," she said, turning towards him, "what makes you think those people know anything about what's going on halfway around the world? You heard them describe their life, right? They barely know what's going on in the rest of Chicago. Their world is this neighborhood. They hang with their people, go to church and school with their people, shop with their people. You name it. Put a dome over this neighborhood and they'd be happy."

"Well," he said, "they seem like a nice family."

"Yeah, they're nice. All of them are nice. Don't mean a thing. You heard how they stammered coming over here. Never put off today what you can put off until tomorrow."

"They're brave," he said.

"Scary us," she said.

They both laughed. Each had two empty lemonade glasses in their hands as they walked up the steps shoulder to shoulder.

"White people," she said. "They probably never sat on a colored person's porch before. I'm just happy they drank my lemonade."

Willowby was about to pick up the chairs and take them inside but Sheila stopped him. "Might as well leave them out," she said, "Michael and Gabriel will be here soon enough."

"Right," said Willowby. He looked one more time across the street, saw the Pedersens were inside their house, and never noticed Carl Bensema, sitting in the shadows on his front porch next door.

ELEVEN

Folks up and down Green Street wondered how a young Black couple was able to afford buying the Clement house. More than a few wondered why they wanted to. People knew the stories: Fifty years before the Jacksons' move, a Black boy had been beaten to death when a raft he was floating on crossed an imaginary line between Black and white beaches on Lake Michigan, prompting a summer of race riots. That boy violated what everyone knew: Chicago lived with defined lines designed to keep Black people in their place. To the neighbors up and down Green Street, the Jacksons' crossing Halsted Street was a foolish violation of this code.

What the neighborhood didn't appreciate was that Sheila and Willowby were fully aware of what they were doing. They had raised funds from church members and a network of Black businesses and then paid cash for the Clements' house so no realtors or banks could surprise them and block the sale. Even though Chicago's redlining neighborhood covenant laws had been deemed illegal, there were too many recent stories of dark-skinned people being shut out of homes in predominantly white neighborhoods for the Jacksons to relax before the deal was completed. The Greater Freedom Methodist Church wanted a place for their pastor in Englewood, and the Black business owners who contributed knew a cash sale would be the smartest way to help this brave young couple in their pioneering choice of location. They understood the risk the Jacksons were taking, so much so that arrangements had been made: after sundown, two men, whom Sheila had named Michael and Gabriel, sat on folding chairs keeping vigil on the Jacksons' front porch. She imagined them out there like archangels over the Ark of the Covenant. If a car passed by the house slowly, they rose to make their presence known.

The next morning as folks came out to collect the *Tribune*, Carl Bensema spread the word up and down Green Street that the Pedersens had actually gone across the street to visit the Jacksons. Carl had made it a point not to speak with his new neighbors. Florence said 'hi' once but Carl quickly reprimanded her. He would scowl at the Jacksons whenever the opportunity arose. Willowby would see them and say, "Greetings, neighbors," and Carl would glare. On occasion, Florence would smile back without Carl noticing.

The Green Street Boys had heard their parents talking about the Pedersens visiting the Jacksons, and on the porch that afternoon they pressed Erik to tell them about it. Erik didn't have much of a story to tell, but decided to act as if he was privy to mounds of detail yet sworn to secrecy. Kristen came walking out the door, and Eddie immediately asked her about the Jacksons. She blew Erik's story by saying they didn't know much at all, that their parents had spent more time with them than they had, and their parents didn't have much to say.

"Don't believe you, Kristen," Frank said from the far side of the porch. "You two know everything about them. Come on, Erik, give it up. What's the big deal? We won't tell anyone."

Kristen was looking at her brother when Pete said, "Friends don't keep secrets. If there's nothing to it, just say so. I think you're scared of something. That's it."

"I bet you were afraid of them, weren't you? Were you?" Frank said as he moved to the center of the porch.

"Yeah, what are they like?" Eddie said. "Do they talk funny?"

"They don't talk funny and they're not scary," Erik said, standing now in the middle of the porch. "What's the matter with you guys? They're just people. I know that he's a pastor. He seems like a nice guy. And she's a teacher at Lindblom. Probably more brains in their pinkies than you three lunkheads put together!"

Kristen had been getting ready to go back in the house, but spoke again from the doorway, "Yeah, what's the matter with you guys? We weren't scared 'cause they're not scary. But I don't know, maybe you guys scare easily."

Erik laughed and Eddie said, "I thought we were going to do something today. I didn't come over here to get told off by your sister."

"Me neither," Pete said. "I'm going home."

"So am I," Frank said. Erik said, "Come on, guys," and then shrugged his shoulders and retreated to the side of the porch as Eddie, Pete, and Frank stood and walked down the steps. Before he reached the sidewalk, Frank turned and gave Erik and Kristen the finger.

"Really, Frank?" Erik called after him. "You're giving the finger to my little sister?"

Frank kept walking backwards toward his house while facing the Pedersen porch, smiling with his finger still in the air. A voice made him spin around.

"Put your finger down." It was Old Man Finnegan, watering the barely alive roses at the front of his house, dressed in his familiar uniform, complete with suspenders. "Don't go walking down the street making a sign like that. It's obscene."

"Yes sir," Frank said. "Sorry, sir."

"Don't I know you? You look familiar."

"Who, me?" Frank said, looking around as if there were dozens of other boys to choose from. "I, um, I don't think so. You must be thinking of someone else." He took a few steps closer to the spot on the sidewalk where he was almost past Old Man Finnegan.

"Ya, ya," Old Man Finnegan said. "I seen you before. What's your name?"

Frank paused and thought. "Ed Sullivan," he said. "And I know you're Mr. Finnegan. Good to see you again." He waved. "I guess I better get home now. I'm sure my parents are missing me by now."

"I don't think that's your real name," Old Man Finnegan said. "But listen, just so you know, I'm watering my flowers here, see? Thought you should know that there's nothing at all under my porch that needs watering. You might want to tell that to your buddies."

For the second time that summer, Frank almost peed his pants at Old Man Finnegan's. He looked for a second like he might run back over to the Pedersens and tell Erik, but Old Man Finnegan was staring right at him, so he ran down Green Street toward home.

That evening no neighbors walked over to the Pedersens and asked what their visit with the Jacksons was about. Nor were there any phone calls. The wake for Fred DeVries, scheduled for the next day, might be a time when there would be questions from those who didn't have the nerve to come to the Pedersens directly. Or, perhaps, the Pedersens would be shunned.

"Tomorrow's a big day," Magnus said to Erik and Kristen in the living room just before bedtime that night. They'd been watching *Ben Casey*. "It's going to be important at the wake for Mr. DeVries that you speak to his children. It's important that you say how sorry you are. Your mom and I will talk to Mrs. DeVries and tell her how sorry we are that her husband is gone. It's important to say these things, not just think them."

"I remember the first time I went to a wake as a child," Fenna said. "It was unusual. We were dressed in our Sunday best, and it wasn't a Sunday."

"What's a wake?" Kristen asked. The influence of Chicago's Irish immigrants had inched into the Dutch world here—although the "wake" for Fred DeVries wouldn't be anything like a traditional Irish wake, with days of eating and drinking alongside a coffin in a house. A Dutch Chicago wake would be called "visitation" in other places—people would stand in line to give their condolences to Fred's wife and children.

"A wake is the time when people who knew the dead person, or know the dead person's family, come to pay their respects," Fenna said. "It's at the funeral home."

"Is his body going to be there?" Kristen asked.

"Yes," Fenna said. "I imagine it will be."

"Do I have to touch it?"

Fenna smiled and said, "No," and then added, "but the members of Mr. DeVries's family might do that."

"That sounds weird," Erik said. "I don't want to touch a dead body."

"It's important we respect them," Magnus said.

"Are people going to be crying?" Erik asked. Then he thought about it and said, "I guess they will be."

"Sure they will," Fenna said. "This is a terrible tragedy." She looked at her children. "Right now, you kids need to go to bed. You're not just asking questions to stay up, are you?" Erik and Kristen nodded and headed for their bedrooms.

Magnus turned to Fenna and said, "We have to prepare them." Yet they never could have prepared their kids fully for all that would happen at Fred DeVries's wake.

Twelve

Each long-established ethnic group in Englewood had its own funeral home: The Bergsma Funeral Home served the Dutch community, the Ryan Funeral Home served the Irish, and the Hansen Funeral Parlor served the Scandinavians.

In its long history, the Bergsma Home had never had a line of visitors trailing out the entrance door north down Halsted Street for a half a block until the wake for Fred DeVries. Not only were those from Grace Christian Reformed Church and Englewood Christian School present, many who had their milk delivered by Fred came to pay their respects to his wife Eleanor and their four children.

It was a hot muggy August afternoon that seemed to bake those waiting to enter the funeral home. In the days following the murder, conversations in both the white and Black neighborhoods had simmered with speculation about who had shot Fred DeVries. No arrests had been made, which added to the emotional weight among those waiting in line.

Kristen and Erik saw plenty of other kids they recognized. The unease of being in an adult world with a dead body waiting at the end of the line was relieved somewhat by knowing they weren't alone.

Kristen was dressed in her Sunday dress and Mary Jane shoes, with silk socks crowned with lace, and a tiny patent leather purse at her side. She stepped out to see how far back the line extended and spotted their new neighbor, the Reverend Willowby Jackson, near the end of the line. She turned back and tugged on her mother's arm, pointing north up Halsted: "He's here. Back there in line! Can't miss him. He's dressed in black with a white line around his neck."

Fenna stepped out of line and looked. Willowby waved and she waved back. Others in line turned to see what was so interesting, their heads moving like a line of dominoes falling in sequence.

It took the Pedersens half an hour to pass through the doors. Willowby waited nearly an hour. After Fenna signed the guest book, each of the Pedersens picked up a memorial card with a picture of Fred on one side and these words from the Heidelberg Catechism on the other:

> Question One: What is your only comfort in life and in death?
>
> Answer: That I, with body and soul, both in life and death, am not my own, but belong unto my faithful Savior Jesus Christ; who with his precious blood has fully satisfied for all my sins, and delivered me from all the power of the devil; and so preserves me that without the will of my heavenly Father not a hair can fall from my head; yea, that all things must be subservient to my salvation, wherefore by His Holy Spirit, He also assures me of eternal life, and makes me heartily willing and ready, henceforth, to live unto Him.

Erik looked at the card, elbowed his sister, and said, "Just like a baseball card without the wrapper and gum." She rolled her eyes.

The furnishings inside the funeral home were more ornate than any Erik and Kristen had seen before, even at their Aunt Evelyn's house. Everything in her living room was covered in plastic—slippery in the winter and sticky on humid summer days. At the Bergsma Funeral home, deep burgundy velvet drapes flanked curtains covering brick walls, creating the effect of windows where there weren't any. Floral wallpaper and plaster-cast plaques hung from the walls. One of the plaques said, "And we know that all things work together for good to them that love God." Erik hoped Mrs. DeVries hadn't spotted it—it didn't make much sense at a time like this.

Erik and Kristen weren't the only ones impressed with the décor; they overhead an adult say, "They even have Oriental rugs." The carpets had elaborate patterns in an array of colors. In one back corner an elderly woman softly played hymns on an organ, and the room was full of flowers and their fragrant scent.

As they moved further in, Erik could see the DeVries family standing side by side at the end of the long line. Near the immediate family, seated in large, overstuffed chairs, were elderly folks who Erik assumed must have been more DeVries relatives. And there was Mr. DeVries, inside a shiny wooden coffin. His hands were folded across his chest and the rest of his body was tucked under part of the coffin's lid. That part of the coffin acted as a ledge—there was a Bible on it and when they got close enough Erik could see it was open to Psalm 23, with a flower carefully placed in the seam like a bookmark. The lid of the coffin had two parts, so half could be open and half could be closed. Erik had seen a door like this on television—Mr. Ed, the talking horse, had a door like that on his stall. Erik had no idea this was called a Dutch door. As they got close, Erik could see that inside the coffin, tucked in next to Mr. DeVries's shoulder, was an empty milk bottle, exactly like those Mr. DeVries had faithfully delivered over all those years.

Erik tried to imagine how he would feel if it were Magnus in the coffin and what it would be like to stand there all afternoon having people say things to you. He imagined it would be terrible. He could hear adults speaking to Mrs. DeVries: "He's in a better place, we know." "God is in control. He has his reasons." "At least he didn't suffer. He didn't, did he?" He watched as Mrs. DeVries greeted everyone and bore whatever it was they had to say. A very old lady with so much makeup on she looked like a corpse herself said, "It looks just like him, dear. They do such a good job here." A young man who Erik knew was a deacon at their church approached Mrs. DeVries, shrugged his shoulders, and then couldn't come up with any words. He blubbered and then hugged Mrs. DeVries and she held his hand for a long time, which seemed to comfort the deacon. He walked away red-faced.

When the Pedersens approached, Magnus held Erik by the shoulders and stood Erik in front of him. Fenna did the same with Kristen. "Our family is so very sorry for your loss, Eleanor," Magnus said. "Fred was a good man, a true saint. We're not saying anything you don't know, but we mean it. He'll be missed by so many." Fenna didn't speak but gave Mrs. DeVries a big hug and held on to her hands.

In the quiet, Mrs. DeVries spoke: "Thank you for coming and for your words," she said. "I'm still in shock, I don't really know what to say or think. I do know he won't be forgotten. Pray for my kids. They already miss him so much."

"We'll be sure to do that," Magnus said, looking straight at Mrs. DeVries.

Kristen approached Mrs. DeVries and said, "I'm very sorry that you lost." Eleanor DeVries looked puzzled for a moment and then stooped to look eye level at Kristen, and said "Sweetie, that's exactly how it feels. Like we lost. Thank you."

Magnus and Fenna stayed with Erik and Kristen as they moved to greet the four DeVries children, who shook their heads and mumbled, "Thanks for coming." Erik felt genuinely sorry that they had to stand there all afternoon talking to all the people.

Magnus ushered the family to a row of padded folding chairs in a section of the expansive room where they could watch the line of people come to pay their respects. Magnus leaned toward his wife and whispered, "We should stay to see Willowby come through."

Erik looked around to see if any of the Green Street Boys were in line, hoping beyond hope that they were. There would be plenty to talk about on the porch. He was sure Eddie and Pete had to be there at some point, maybe even Frank. As he looked, he saw Simon De Bolt. He looked around but didn't see the Reverend Wolthuis. Kristen poked him hard in the ribs and whispered, "I think it moved. He must be alive."

"What are you talking about?"

"The milk bottle, stupid. Stare at it when people pass by. I saw it move. I know it did."

"There's no way he's alive," Erik half-whispered. "If he was, do you think he'd stay there with all that makeup on? Just shut up and pay your respects in quiet."

He never did see any of the Green Street Boys, but after a while Willowby Jackson entered the room. Erik watched him sign the guest book, take a memorial card, and stand with his hands folded in front of him. There was sweat shining on his forehead. Erik looked around and could see Willowby was the only Black person in the funeral home.

When the time came for Willowby to greet Eleanor DeVries he reached into his suit pocket and pulled out a small black leather

Bible. Erik was close enough to hear him say, "Mrs. DeVries, my name is Reverend Willowby Jackson. I've come here on behalf of my church, the Greater Freedom Methodist Church. Many of our members knew and loved your husband. May I read a scripture passage to you that brings me comfort?" When she nodded yes, Willowby read: "Then I saw a new heaven and a new earth, for the first heaven and the first earth had passed away. And I heard a loud voice from the throne saying, Look! God's dwelling place is now among the people, and he will dwell with them. They will be his people, and God himself will be with them and be their God. He will wipe away every tear from their eyes. There will be no more death or mourning or crying in pain, for the old order of things has passed away. I am making everything new." He finished and then added, "May I say one more thing?"

She gave a slight nod.

"There is unfinished business here. I speak for myself and my congregation. We pray that justice will come and those who took your husband's rich life will be found and held to account. I want you and your family to know this. God bless you now and in the days ahead." With that he walked to the Pedersens and shook their hands, slowly and firmly. They stared after him as he made his way toward the door.

Willowby was heading toward the door when Luke Siebenga, a nineteen-year-old friend of the oldest DeVries boy, called after him. "Hey Reverend, come back here."

Willowby turned and stood where he was. Luke, who matched Willowby in size and height, approached him. "Who invited you here? It was your kind who killed my friend's dad. Cold-blooded killed him. You have your nerve showing up here like this, stirring things up." Luke's hands were curled into fists. "I mean, look at you," he said. "You come here dressed like a priest, spouting the Bible and all. Are you trying to start something?"

Willowby held his hands up in front of his chest. "I meant no harm, son, with either my words or my dress." He paused and breathed deeply: "This white collar stands for something. It's a sort of a billboard for God. It opens doors, like this one. I came to speak words of comfort and peace. My apologies if that's not how they appeared to you. I meant them sincerely."

"Why don't you just leave?" Luke said.

"That's what I was doing," Willowby said. He walked through the crowd with his head held high, slowly heading for the door, where Ben Bergsma, the funeral director, stood. Ben Bergsma offered Willowby a handshake and opened the door to Halsted and sunlight. Willowby took a deep breath, sighed, and headed home.

A group of people surrounded the Pedersens. Carl Bensema said, "That's the guy who moved in next door, who lives across the street from you." Magnus looked up wearily and Carl said, "See what happens when you try to get to know them?"

"He's a very nice man," Magnus said.

"I hope God strikes the son of a bitch dead," Carl said.

Magnus said, "Please, Carl, my children are here."

"Just look at what you're doing," Carl said, almost mutilating Fred DeVries's memorial card in his hand.

The Pedersens walked home slowly without speaking. Erik started to say something but Magnus gave him a look which said this wasn't the time. Magnus and Fenna held hands as they walked down Halsted toward home.

Finally, Kristen broke the silence: "I think Reverend Wolthuis should wear one of those collars, like Mr. Jackson does. He could be more of a billboard."

Erik noticed a hint of a smile on his mom and dad's faces.

Thirteen

Englewood Christian School served kindergarten through ninth-grade students. The school had been founded for the covenant children of Dutch immigrants in 1912 as a haven from the worldly tendencies and strange ways of America. Fifty years later, it primarily served the children of the Christian Reformed Church; few other parents in Englewood were willing to pay the tuition required to enroll their children there. "If you're not Dutch, you're not much," was the unspoken underlying assumption behind the school, and denominational officials tended to speak of the Christian school, the church, and the Christian family as the foundational holy triangle required for the successful raising of children.

As August receded and a new school year approached, news began circulating among the Englewood Christian School parents centered on one of the missionaries to Nigeria their church sponsored. Normally, news from or about a missionary was an occasion for joy or celebration. But this news was a different type, unsettling and unusual.

Michael Schaap was an aviation missionary. He flew other missionaries into remote regions where they would spread the gospel. He and his plane were also available for emergency medical issues, when his plane would become a flying ambulance. Schaap's aerial adventures were legendary: he was Billy Graham with wings, or Charles Lindbergh ordained for ministry. On top of all that, he was a son of Englewood. Since Ebenezer Christian Reformed Church had closed and sold its building to the Greater Freedom Methodist Church, Grace Christian Reformed Church had become the main sponsor of Michael Schaap's missionary endeavors. Schaap had been baptized as an infant at Ebenezer, made his profession of faith as a teenager there, and was commissioned there as a young adult for his work in Africa. But now, Grace was his home church. His parents had stayed in Englewood, and when Ebenezer CRC closed, they transferred their membership to Grace.

Every seven years the denominational mission board granted Schaap and other missionaries under their care a furlough, a sabbatical of sorts designed to grant restoration and renewal from the challenging work of a foreign mission field. The fields were full of potential converts, but workers were few, and so missionaries were treated with great respect and admiration.

Schaap, like most missionaries on furlough, drew big crowds at speaking engagements. While Grace Christian Reformed was his home base, he also toured other churches throughout Chicagoland, invited by each congregation's Ladies Missionary Society to special luncheons in church basements. Lunch was usually ham buns and potato salad, and then there would be hymn singing after the Jell-O dessert. Schaap would set up a table displaying snake skins, tools, musical instruments, and native dress for the ladies to marvel at and touch. The highlight of the event was a narrated slide show depicting close calls on primitive airfields, imminent danger surrounding native villages, and photos of joyful saved native souls singing songs in English from used hymnals shipped from these very churches.

Michael began his service in Nigeria as an unmarried man fresh out of flight school, eager to be a vital part of the missionary effort. Before long he met and married a Nigerian woman named Ruth, a name she'd chosen when she converted to Christianity, who had captivated him with her warmth and wit and easy conversation. She was a nurse who, at times, had been a passenger on his plane. Ruth and Michael had two children, Naomi and Benjamin. When they grew to school age, they attended a Christian school for children of missionary families in Jos, where Naomi and Benjamin stood out from their white-skinned and blond-haired schoolmates. To their classmates, the Schaap children looked more like the "unwashed heathens" their parents had come to save than covenant children like themselves.

Now the Schaap family was coming to the United States for a year, and, with the help of Mel Lamsma, the Christian Reformed Church Mission Board had secured an apartment for the Schaaps above the Bruinius grocery store across the street from the Englewood Christian School. Word was spreading through Englewood that the Schaap children would enroll there. They would be the first Black students in the history of Englewood Christian School.

Michael was eager to come home and the Schaap children were excited about living in Chicago, but Ruth had sleepless nights. The night before they were to leave for Chicago, her feelings finally tumbled out: "I wish I was more settled about this move, Michael." After dinner that evening, Ruth said, "I'm worried. You're much more eager than I am for what's ahead. A year seems like such a long time."

Michael looked at her and started to say something, but she spoke again.

"Your parents are the only people I'll know," she said, "and I've only known them for the little time they were at our wedding. One week. That's it."

"My parents will be great," he said. "So will everyone else. I know this is all new, but I don't think there's much to worry about." He got up and lazily washed out their supper dishes.

Ruth stood and touched his arm: "Michael, there's a lot to worry about."

"I'm sorry," he said, "but America is great. Chicago is great. And our kids need to know they're both American and Nigerian."

"Let's go back and sit at the table," Ruth said. "I want you to listen to me." He took a deep breath and sat down across from her. The kids were in another room, looking through their suitcases one last time.

"It's great for you," Ruth said, "because you're one of them. More than that, you're their hero. But I have read the newspapers. I know about the sit-ins in America at lunch counters and I've read about the freedom riders in the south part of America, and church bombings and things. I don't know if Chicago is any better, or worse. Look at my skin, Michael. Tell me it won't be a problem. Tell me loneliness won't be my companion."

Michael reached for her hands. "I really don't know how things will go for us, for you, for the kids," he said. "I've thought about it. I just didn't bring it up because I didn't want to give you more to worry about."

"I am scared," she said.

"So am I," he said, "but not scared enough to let fear stop us."

Two weeks after the DeVries funeral, on a Saturday afternoon, a large crowd gathered at Midway Airport to welcome the Schaaps. The family's trip was long—Lagos to London, London to New York, and then on to Chicago in a small prop jet. Their plane was late arriving in Chicago, but the curiosity in the crowd was undiminished.

The welcoming party was a fair representation of the church and school community. The Reverend Wolthuis came in full ministerial garb: suit and tie and wingtip shoes, as if this were a gathering of the saints on a Sunday morning. He was accompanied by Simon De Bolt, who could have been mistaken for a folk singer in his blue jeans with the cuffs rolled up and wide-striped shirt. His casual attire reflected his position: in a few days, his internship would end and he'd return to seminary for his senior year.

The long-awaited plane, a TWA Constellation with the unmistakable triple-tail, flew low and landed, circled at the end of the runway and made its way to the terminal, where a staircase was rolled out for the passengers to exit. The welcoming party scurried to the entrance below and watched as the Schaaps disembarked. They would be easy to spot.

"Who do you think the children will look like? The father or mother?" Marge Koning asked no one in particular.

"I'm guessing they have some kind of accent, that's what I'm thinking," said Evelyn Medema, who was standing nearby. Some of the women brought baked goods. Others brought flowers. Carl Bensema was dragged to the airport against his will by his wife and skulked in a corner of the waiting room, smoking in defiance. He said he'd come only because he liked airplanes. When the Pedersens arrived, Erik had seen Eddie Medema and Pete Koning, and they received permission to go to the observation deck to watch the landing.

When the Schaaps entered the terminal, Ruth saw nothing but white faces. She'd seen Black people handling luggage in New York, but this was a sea of white. Michael stepped forward and started shaking hands and greeting people, while she stood back.

"Ruth," Michael said, "these are the Pedersens. You know them—they write us and send me news about the White Sox."

Ruth looked them over and saw a girl hugging the leg of her mother. The little girl reached out and touched Ruth's daughter Naomi, who smiled.

"It's a pleasure to make your acquaintance, ma'am," Ruth said.

"What?" Fenna said. "I'm sorry, I don't understand you."

Ruth spoke again, saying the same words more slowly and loudly.

Fenna understood this time and said, "We want you to know that we will do what we can to make your stay here comfortable and welcoming."

"If you want to help us," Ruth said, "show me the W.C."

"The what?" Fenna asked.

"The W.C. The water closet. It's been a long trip." Beside her, Michael was putting his hands up to get the crowd's attention.

"Friends, and brothers and sisters in Christ," he said, "I speak for myself and Ruth, and our children Naomi and Benjamin, in thanking you for this warm welcome. We started yesterday in Nigeria and after three long flights we are finally here. They were good flights, almost as good as if I had been flying the planes myself!" Everyone laughed.

Fenna, finally figuring out what Ruth had been asking for, took her arm and showed her the way to the women's room while Michael's speech went on behind her. When she came out, he was still talking, saying something about how good it was to be home. "Here's Ruth," he said, "maybe she'd like to add something."

"Thank you so very much for this kind welcome," she said, speaking her words slowly as she had to Fenna. "The church in Nigeria, where the rest of my family remain, sends its greetings." She paused. "And before long, my children and I would like to try some of those famous hot dogs Michael tells us about." The crowd laughed louder at her joke than they had at Michael's.

"See, I told you she'd have an accent," Evelyn Medema said to Marge Koning.

"And I think the children are definitely African looking, don't you?" Marge said. "If you didn't know they were our people, you might think they were uncivilized."

The Reverend Wolthuis moved to the front of the crowd with a broad smile. "We're so grateful to God for his traveling mercies," he said, "and so eager to have you in our community. Michael and Ruth, we await the good news you bring us about your work in Nigeria. And children, I look forward to seeing you in Sunday school." With that he presented Ruth with a book, wrapped in dull brown paper. "You'll find this to be a helpful guide for your stay here."

"And now," the Reverend Wolthuis said, "let us show God's welcome." With hands raised, he began: "Grace be to you and peace from God the Father, and from our Lord Jesus Christ, who gave himself for our sins, that he might deliver us from this present evil world, according to the will of God our Father; to whom be glory forever and ever. Amen."

Simon De Bolt came forward, shook Michael's hand, and said, "The congregation knew you would need a car. We've got a car outside that we purchased for you."

It was a serviceable '52 Chevy automatic, dull grey, complete with a metal line down the middle of the windshield, fresh off a parishioner's used car lot. Serviceable, but Michael wouldn't need to worry about speeding tickets.

Once the family was settled in the car, and the luggage was placed in what Ruth had called "the boot," Ruth unwrapped the book the Revered Wolthuis had handed her. *Divining God's Holy Word: A Devotional* stood out in gold letters against brown leather. The author's name was below the title: The Reverend

Calvin Wolthuis. The book held meditations for every day of the year.

Ruth laughed and showed the book to her husband, who shook his head. "I thought it would be about Chicago," she said.

"Welcome to the Christian Reformed Church," he said.

Before long they arrived at the second-floor apartment across from the Englewood Christian School. It had been filled with used furniture gathered from the homes of church folk. They'd even anticipated a Chicago winter and filled the closets with clothes never needed in Nigeria. Games and sporting equipment for Naomi and Benjamin spread across the bedding in their rooms. It was all very nice, Ruth thought. Nice, all very nice.

Fourteen

Magnus and Fenna were sitting on the porch late one night after the kids had been put to bed when Fenna said, "There's something we need to talk about."

"Something I've done?" Magnus asked, turning toward her.

"No, nothing you've done. More like something you need to do. I was dusting the bookshelf in the front room the other day—long overdue and very dusty, don't know how I let that happen—and I noticed there was no dust in front of my nursing book on anatomy. It was clean as a whistle. I haven't touched that book in years. But someone in this house has." Fenna smiled.

"I didn't look at your book," her husband said. "I prefer the real thing."

"I know you do," Fenna said. "But there is a twelve-year-old boy in this house who might find that book fascinating."

"Yeah, I guess so."

Fenna reached out and touched Magnus on the arm. "So, I was thinking about it and it occurred to me that Erik is in seventh grade. This is the year he gets the famous sex talk at school. You know, the talk no one talks about?"

"That's this year?"

"Yes, this year." Fenna said. "Dr. Hoekstra takes the boys, Dr. Woldman the girls. They don't get very specific from what I hear, mostly what to expect as bodies go through changes at their age. The boys don't learn a thing about girls and vice versa. They expect parents to fill in the blanks."

"Uh-oh," Magnus said.

"I'll talk with Kristen when it's her turn, but you need to talk to Erik. We know he's already wondering, or he wouldn't be sneaking my book."

A couple of days later, Fenna told Kristen that since school was starting the next week, she needed to head to bed a bit earlier so she could start adjusting to her school bedtime. Magnus and Erik stayed on the porch, with the pink sunset showing through the phone lines and over the rooftops as they looked west across the street. They sat next to each other on the top stair and waved when they saw Gabriel and Michael arrive to sit on the Jacksons' front porch.

Normally, Magnus and Erik would listen to a White Sox game or police calls on the transistor radio, but Magnus had placed the radio on the small table by the front door so they wouldn't be distracted. "So Erik," Magnus said, "There's something we need to talk about, father to son, man to man."

Erik looked at his dad. "What?"

"Well, something important."

"What?"

His dad stood, wiped his hands on his pants, looked at his son, and then sat down again next to him. "Well, there's no point in beating around the bush. I'll tell you straight out: we need to talk about sex."

Erik looked around for a moment. "Wait, what? Are you sure? I mean, maybe we should wait until I pubertize," Erik said, eyebrows raised in the shape of fear.

Magnus took a couple of deep breaths. "You see," he said, "that's a good place to start. The word is puberty. That's an example of why we should have this talk. Just to get things straight, see, say, if you have questions, you know, any questions at all, so you don't have to wonder about what sex is all about. Okay?"

"Well, yeah. I suppose so." Erik interlaced his fingers together and then pulled them apart. He wished he had been warned about this.

His father kept talking, telling Erik about what was going to happen when Dr. Hoekstra visited school. While Magnus talked, Erik's mind raced at the mention of girls. He looked past his father at the second floor of the apartment next door, where the lovely Doris Eck lived with her long legs and killer smile. Sometimes, while he was sitting in his treehouse, she'd wave at Erik from her second-floor rear porch. He was pretty sure he was in love with Doris Eck.

Magnus brought Erik back to the conversation. "Let's start at the beginning. Before we even talk about bodies or anatomy, I want to talk with you about respecting women."

Well, Erik thought, I'm on pretty solid ground there. I respect Doris Eck. A lot.

"I don't know if you have ever noticed," Magnus said, "but I try to treat your mother—well, all women really—with respect and politeness. I always try to remember that whoever we meet in whatever situation, is someone made in the image of God. Everyone should be treated with respect and honor."

Erik had heard that kind of language before, in sermons and in catechism classes and at Englewood Christian. And he had noticed that his dad did things like holding doors open, and walking ahead in revolving doors, and once Magnus had told him that if he was walking with a girl he should walk on the curb side of the sidewalk in case cars splashed puddles. He wasn't sure what that had to do with sex.

"Here's another example about respect," Magnus continued, "you know how it bothers me when one of your friends calls his father the 'Old Man'?"

Erik nodded, confident that they weren't talking about sex anymore. "Oh! Yeah, don't worry Dad. I never would say that about you," Erik said. "Or moron. Or idiot. That's what Frank calls his dad." And to make sure Magnus knew he got the meaning of the conversation, he said, "Like when the Konings come to our house on Sunday nights for coffee and Mr. Koning uses the n-word. Right? Like that?"

"Well, yes," Magnus said, "very much the same thing. Clearly disrespectful and dishonoring."

"That's image of God stuff too, right?" Erik said.

"Yes, exactly. Image of God. Glad you see the connection."

"So, what does Mr. Koning say when you correct him?" Erik asked. "You correct him, right?"

Magnus shifted his weight and cleared his throat: "Well, to be honest, that's a tough one. Sorry to say I don't correct him. Haven't yet, at least. Probably should. But I get what you're driving at, Erik, and you're right to ask me."

Erik rested his chin on his knees, still wondering where all of this was going.

"So, okay, respect for image bearers of God. That's where we start," Magnus said. "And sometimes it's the little things. Like holding doors open for women. Just little gestures of respect. Not just to be nice or because she's weak. You know your mother doesn't need me to open doors."

"So why don't you hold doors open for men? They're image bearers too, right? Would you hold a door open for Uncle Mick?" Erik asked.

"And get punched in the mouth?" Magnus laughed, then sensed that Erik sincerely wondered. "Yes, even Uncle Mick is an image bearer. It's important to remember that when people frustrate us."

"I want to see you hold a door for Uncle Mick."

"It doesn't matter if it's Uncle Mick or President Kennedy or Tony Spilotro," Magnus said.

Erik smiled at the mention of Tony the Ant, Chicago's mafia boss, the 1960s version of Al Capone. Magnus reached over and affectionately ruffled his son's hair. "Maybe I should stick my head inside and see if your mother might bring us a couple of glasses of water."

Erik felt relief. They weren't talking about sex at all. At least not sex like the Green Street Boys talked about it. Stuff like getting to first base. He was pretty sure he'd been to first base when he kissed Sally Kostelyk at last year's Halloween costume party, sneaking it in while bobbing for apples with her. Second base, third base, and home runs were the stuff of speculation among the Boys; no one had any clarity on the matter but all agreed talking about the possibilities was exciting.

The Green Street Boys talked about sex all the time. Frank Bertolli remained hopelessly fixated on Annette Funicello. Pete Koning was fond of sharing that he had a boner whenever he spotted Priscilla De Haan on the playground at school or on the sidewalk outside church on Sundays. Eddie Medema confessed that he regularly checked the treasure trove of *Playboy* magazines hidden under the front seat of the cartage truck parked in his parents' garage, space rented out to a friend from church. Every so often the Boys made their way to Eddie's house and smuggled a few copies for viewing under the Rock Island train bridge along 76th Street, never suspecting the origin of these pages of sensual delight was in an office a few blocks away from Erik's father's office in downtown Chicago.

And Erik was absolutely smitten by Kathy Lennon, the youngest of the Lennon Sisters who sang on *The Lawrence Welk Show*. Magnus liked to talk about "the happy Norwegian," Myron Floren, the accordionist with the permanent smile who accompanied the orchestra. But Kathy Lennon was why Erik watched. There was just something about her smile that said she was nice. She seemed like someone he could take out for a milkshake and maybe get to first base with. He wasn't sure how sex or love worked, but was pretty sure he was in love with both Doris Eck and Kathy Lennon at the same time. Was that a sin? Erik didn't know, but it didn't feel wrong and, on top of that, he'd heard of guys in the Bible with lots of wives. Solomon had a few hundred wives, and he was supposed to be the wisest person ever. If it was good enough for Solomon, it was good enough for Erik.

A lot of the time the Green Street Boys would joke about sexual stuff Erik didn't really get, but he'd laugh anyway. Pete insisted the line "Here I raise my Ebenezer" in the hymn "Come Thou Fount of Every Blessing" was about some guy in the olden days getting a boner (for all Erik knew, it might have been Solomon), and Erik and Pete and Eddie would laugh and look around for each other in church whenever they sang that song. But they'd laugh at other stuff in church that didn't have anything to do with sex, like the Lord's Prayer beginning, "Our father, who art in heaven, Harold be thy name." Even Catholic Frank got that joke.

Fenna had brought them water, and they'd both had a sip and set their glasses beside them on the porch. "Erik," Magnus said. Erik turned and looked directly at his father. "Look, I know this is probably awkward for us to talk about right now, so how about this? Let's agree that your body is changing, you're interested in girls, and they're changing too, and someday you'll start wanting to go out on dates with them. We'll leave the mechanics of puberty and sex to Dr. Hoekstra. You listen carefully, and you let me know if you have any questions. What do you think? Sound like a plan?"

With a great sigh of relief, Erik said, "Sounds good. I like this man-to-man stuff. And Dad, after I listen to Dr. Hoekstra, if you have questions, don't be afraid to ask." He poked Magnus on the shoulder, and his dad laughed. Magnus stood, stretched, and after waving at the men on the Jacksons' porch, Erik picked up their water glasses and Magnus led his son into their home.

Fifteen

The Englewood Christian School Board met monthly in the school band room, the room with the most windows that allowed for air circulation in summer months and ventilation for cigarette and cigar smoke year-round. Despite the open windows, a dozen bangs on the timpani would send tobacco odors wafting through the room, and kids who played a wind instrument would complain of a strange taste in their mouth the day after a board meeting.

Like the governing councils of the Christian Reformed Churches, which founded and supported the school, the board was all men, made up of representatives from the school's supporting churches. The school couldn't exist without the churches—each supporting church financially supplemented the tuition paid by the parents who sent their children to the school. Even with this help, the commitment to paying tuition was a burden for school parents, but the Dutch Reformed weren't the only community to do it: Englewood's Lutheran and Catholic parents paid to send their children to their own private schools, too.

Sam Slager, proprietor of Slager Shoes on Halsted Street, served as the Englewood School Board president. The parents of Englewood Christian School were his customers—unless there was a bargain to be found at Sears. Unlike Sears, where shoe-shopping was practically self-serve, Sam would carefully measure foot sizes and help his customers get just the right fit. Sears didn't carry extra-wide or extra-long sizes like Sam did, but shoes at Sears were less expensive, so thrift battled comfort in a constant war on the feet of the Dutch residents of Englewood. Thrift claimed more victories.

School had been in session for two weeks when the board met in late September, and overall things were looking good. As baptismal records had predicted, enrollment was up slightly, and three of the four new teachers had started the year quite nicely. They were new to Englewood Christian, but were experienced educators, having taught most recently in public schools. A fourth teacher was fresh out of college and was struggling as the year opened.

"It's the same old story," Principal Rodney Hoekema informed the board. "She's young and wants to be their friend. It's like throwing chum overboard—soon the sharks will be circling." He promised—as he'd done often over the years with new teachers—to be vigilant and sit in on her class regularly. "I'm sure Miss Van Der Sloot will work out," the principal added. "Grand Rapids doesn't produce duds." He paused and said, "I should know. That's where I grew up. She's got a good head on her shoulders and will learn to keep things in check."

The next item on the agenda had to do with questions about the orthodoxy of the Bible teacher, and the question was raised by Henk Koning. "Mr. Chairman," he said, looking at Sam Slager. "I've heard some odd things about this teacher. I hear he's introducing evolution as established fact."

Slager looked at Rodney Hoekema, who jumped in again. "We've got nothing to worry about," the principal said. "Maurice Van Den Bosch is right as rain. Yes, he has mentioned evolution in the classroom. It would be irresponsible if he did not. How else will our children know what the world thinks and what's being taught in the godless public schools? But Maury sets it side-by-side with Adam and Eve and asks the boys and girls to choose who they want to be descended from—apes, or men and women? Our children have the good sense to choose Adam and Eve. Their parents raise them well." A sense of relief travelled through the room and Henk Koning nodded with satisfaction.

Next on the agenda was a follow-up to a special board meeting a few weeks earlier to consider the enrollment application of the Schaap children. The board had not been of one mind. After considerable debate and with pockets of misgiving, the board decided by a slim majority to admit them on the grounds that, although half-Black, they were also half-white. The case in their favor had been made that they were indeed children of the covenant—they had been baptized and claimed by God as his own. Not everyone was ready to affirm that, and now that school was in session, questions were posed about how the presence of the Schaap children was impacting the school, and whether there were negative responses from the school community.

Principal Hoekema addressed the issue: "Let me begin," he said, "by asking you gentlemen to imagine what it might be like for you to be young again and transported to Nigeria to attend school. A school where you were the only white child. Keep that in mind while I address your questions." Rodney Hoekema had taught for many years, and when he taught, he liked to walk around his classroom. He stood now, stepped away from his chair, and paced around the band room.

"From an educational point of view," he said, "the Schaap children are doing quite well. They came to Englewood from a good school. They are, it appears, very bright, and they seem eager to learn. But it should not surprise you that, socially, it may take some time to adjust. Teachers report that although they are not picked on for being different, not many friendships have been formed yet. They often seek each other out at recess periods, and stand by themselves. It's early yet, but we hope some of our students will befriend them before long." He had wandered to the far end of the band room and absentmindedly picked up a drumstick.

"But there is something else you should know. I have received more than a few hostile letters about our decision to admit Naomi and Benjamin. Most of these letters are anonymous. My sense is that some are from our own constituents. Others likely come from the broader community, from people who know very little about our school. They only know that we have admitted Negro students. These letters are filled with anger. Some are completely vulgar. There are no threats of violence. Yet." He looked at the drumstick like he was an archeologist making a discovery, and then quickly put it down.

Sam Slager lit a cigarette as the principal returned to his seat and his words settled. After a deep drag, the chairman exhaled and then looked around to ask his fellow board members, "What are you hearing?"

"Maybe we made a mistake," the realtor Mel Lamsma said. "I'm thinking of the best interests of all the students, of course."

"Of course you are," Meine Decker said. "But I can't get my mind off us going to school in Nigeria. I am thinking of me in a leopard skin and Mel in a grass skirt. Me Tarzan. Him Mel." Everyone laughed but Mel.

"Look," Mel said, "this is no joke. We are the school board, and the safety and welfare of our children is in our hands. The community expects us to do the right thing to protect our children. If harm should come to any of them ... we simply cannot have blood on our hands. Let's not kid ourselves—there are nutcases out there, and at the least we ought to consider asking for regular police patrols at the beginning and end of the school day."

"I will contact the police," Rodney Hoekema said, "and inform them of the letters, and request a regular presence around the school building." After he had spoken, he made a point of looking up at the band room clock.

"Mr. Hoekema," Sam Slager said, "we trust you with this. You have the wisdom for such a time as this, and may the Lord give you what you need to weather any storm you may face. We thank you for your leadership. Now, the hour is getting late. Before we adjourn, is there any new business?"

A few members started shuffling their papers together, preparing to leave, when another spoke. "You gentlemen know I'm a member of Covenant CRC," Hannes Piersma, who rarely spoke in board meetings, said. His church, Covenant CRC, was located at 70th and Emerald, the border of Englewood's Black/white divide. "In case you haven't heard, at our last council meeting we formed a property search committee. We've been losing folks for a while who are moving out to the southwest suburbs. Our property search team is looking in Evergreen Park and Oak Lawn. Maybe even Roseland, here in the city.

Mel Lamsma spoke again: "This is news to me, but I'm not surprised to hear it. No one knows how folks are worried about their property values better than me."

"I should add one more thing," Hannes Piersma said, "this is not for public broadcast. We don't want rumors flying around. I trust you to keep this quiet."

"Then why tell us?" Meine Decker asked.

"Isn't it obvious?" Henk Koning said. "We should be thinking about doing the same thing."

"With our churches?" Meine asked. "Or with the school? Or with our houses?" He looked around the table, trying to read the faces of his fellow board members.

"You're a fool if you're not thinking about this with your house," Mel Lamsma said. "But I imagine Hannes is telling us because we're the school board and we ought to be doing the same."

"Mr. Chairman," Henk Koning said, "I make a motion to appoint a property search committee to investigate a future location for Englewood Christian School."

"Support," Mel Lamsma said.

"Just a minute," Meine said. "Let's not be hasty." He looked around the table. "We have our lives and our businesses here. Sam, if we ditch this community, you're going to have to start over someplace new, and good luck getting on a street with the traffic of Halsted."

There was silence for a bit, and then Arie Vos, the longest serving board member, spoke: "Mr. Chairman," he said, "I make a motion to postpone the previous motion until our next meeting. It's late, this is important, and we need time to think this through and talk this through."

"Support," said Meine Decker.

Sam Slager looked at Henk Koning, who nodded in agreement. The motion carried and after a closing prayer from Principal Rodney Hoekema, the board members walked out silently until they reached the sidewalk, lit cigarettes forming clouds of smoke above them. Conversations outside lingered for nearly thirty minutes, and a few adjourned to Donegan's Tavern to continue the discussion.

Most board members were home and fast asleep around midnight when a few sticks of dynamite, placed on a rear window ledge of the band room, blew a hole in the side of the building large enough to drive a school bus through. The explosion was heard and felt throughout Englewood, and the police were on the scene within minutes. Sirens wailed, and soon a crowd of people in pajamas, robes, boxer shorts, and slippers lined Sangamon Street to watch the fire crew snuff the flames.

The Pedersens scurried the four blocks to the school to join the growing crowd. There was smoke in the air and water flooded the ground around the building's foundation. Flashing lights atop fire trucks and squad cars reflected off the windows of the homes across the street, including the apartment above the store where the Schaap family lived. They too were on the street, wrapped in blankets, eyes glued to the action at their doorstep.

As the Pedersens took in the scene, Kristen tugged at her mom's arm and said, "Look, he's here." Fenna looked and saw her brother-in-law, Mick O'Rourke, standing on the sidewalk doing crowd control.

Kristen tapped her brother and said, "Over there," and pointed in Mick's direction. "Let's go talk to him." Kristen took Erik's arm, but he twisted his arm out of her grip.

"I don't want to talk to him," Erik said. Magnus and Fenna walked over to Mick with Kristen but Erik stayed back. Mick stood facing the crowd, arms extended to keep the bystanders back, occasionally looking over his shoulder at the action around the school.

"Mick, hey Mick, what can you tell us?" Magnus asked. "This is our kids' school."

"Magnus, what d'ya say? What's up, Fenna?" Mick said. "Didn't see you standing there." He didn't look at Kristen or look for Erik. "I just got here, really, but I did get a look around back. A bomb or somethin' like that. Dynamite maybe. Blew a big hole in a classroom wall on the back of the building, ground level."

"Dynamite?" Magnus said. "Who'd do something like that? Why would anyone want to blow up a school?"

Mick took his eyes off the crowd and addressed Magnus directly: "Word is that you got some colored kids at the school now. Is that right?"

Magnus stepped back. "Well, yes, that's right. Two kids here this year. The children of one of our missionaries."

"I suppose this is none of my business," Mick said, dropping his arms and giving Magnus his full attention, "but that sounds like a dumb move to me. Probably should have let the station know."

"You think someone would bomb our school because we have two Negro children here? In Chicago? This isn't Mississippi."

Mick shrugged his shoulders, shifted his considerable weight, and continued to look at his brother-in-law. They stood in silence for a while before Magnus spoke again: "Well, we'll leave you to it, Mick. Take care and say hello to my sister."

As Magnus was turning to walk back to Erik, Mick spoke: "Hey Magnus, again, this is probably none of my business, but what's it gonna take? Beatings. Murder. Now a bomb. Englewood's turnin' to shit. I know my opinion don't matter much to you, but I'd get out while you can."

Magnus stood fully facing Mick and was about to speak when Fenna squeezed her husband's arm. Magnus paused and said, "Englewood needs the police to do their jobs, Mick."

"Why the hell do you think I'm standing out here after midnight, Magnus?" Mick said, turning away to put his arms back up.

The Pedersens were called the next morning before breakfast, informing them school was cancelled for at least the rest of the week. Repairs to the building needed to be made and classes would not begin until engineers certified the building was structurally sound. The FBI was called to handle the investigation, and the school bombing was covered extensively by all the Chicago newspapers. Yet even with all the attention, just like in the beating of George Clement and the murder of Fred DeVries, no suspects emerged.

Sixteen

Carl and Florence Bensema had gotten married a few weeks after they graduated from high school in 1950, moved into an apartment in Englewood, and saved every penny they could to make a down payment on a house. After two years, they had saved $200.

In the years immediately after World War II, Chicago real estate boomed. Between the returning veterans and African Americans coming north for jobs, there simply weren't enough homes. Because of the high demand, home prices in Chicago were among the highest in the nation, and the modest three-bedroom house on Green Street that Carl and Florence had their heart set on listed for just under $10,000. After they toured the house with Mel Lamsma, he explained they would need to be able to put ten percent of the home price down to qualify for a mortgage. Their spirits sank—they were $800 short. Carl had never been accused of being an optimist, and he didn't see how they ever could ever afford to own their own home.

Florence told their tale of woe over dinner at her parents' home one Sunday afternoon, and Florence's father responded by offering to give them $1,000. "Use your $200 on furniture," he said. "Young couples always need furniture, especially baby furniture."

Florence looked at her mother, who was beaming, and then at her father, and said, "I'm not expecting, Daddy."

He also smiled and said, "Once you're settled in your own home I am sure it won't be too long until we hear the pitter patter of little feet around the place."

Florence looked at Carl, who wasn't smiling. "I can't accept a gift like that," Carl said. He looked down at the floor, and said, "I ain't no sponge."

"Then it's a loan," his father-in-law said. This was an act of mercy. There would be no interest and no timetable for repayment of the loan, but calling it a loan made all the difference to Carl. He simply could not take a handout.

Still, he was ashamed of the loan, and in the decade that they'd lived on Green Street, only Carl and Florence and Florence's parents knew about it. Carl forbade Florence to speak of it. Their house was the visible fruit of his hard work and a representation of his manhood, not a sign of his father-in-law's largesse. Word of the loan would make him look weak, and Carl didn't like looking weak.

There were a lot of things Carl didn't like. He worked at the Pullman railcar yard and didn't like it. He'd hired in there soon after leaving high school and watched as others were promoted around him while his job stayed the same. To make it worse, he had to work with Black people. And then there were the White Sox. The one time in his lifetime the White Sox had gotten to the World Series they lost, and now they never hit enough to get over the hump and get back. The White Sox were just like everything else. To Carl, there was no question that the city of Chicago in general and Englewood in particular were falling apart. He didn't have to look far to see evidence of this. It was right next door. The Clements had not been terrible neighbors, though Carl thought both of them were a bit kooky. Carl never really could pinpoint why he never took to them until they sold their house to the Jacksons. Given the reason why the Clements sold their house in the first place, it was the height of irresponsibility to sell it to coloreds. It came to him that the reason he never liked the Clements was because they could not be counted on. George and Millie Clement were unreliable. They had sold their house to the last people in the world they should have sold it to. Now Carl's next-door neighbor was one of them. Jackson could parade around all he wanted dressed up in his fancy clothes looking like he worked for the Pope, but it didn't make him human. Carl's house, his pride and joy, and his family, were being contaminated by what was living next door.

If that wasn't bad enough, there was his bleeding-heart neighbor Pedersen across the street. You sure couldn't count on him either. Carl was certain Pedersen had voted to put a Catholic in the White House. Now Pedersen and his bland wife and spoiled-brat kids had come over and sat on Jackson's porch like they were regular people. Pedersen had never come over and sat on Carl's porch, but he'd sat on that porch. Geez.

On top of it all, the Christian School Board admitted two colored kids to the school, the school his boys attended. The fact they were missionary kids made no difference to Carl. In his mind, this was another step in the wrong direction and a rotten decision by the school board. He had instructed his boys to keep their distance from their new mulatto classmates, but Carl knew more needed to be done. It did not surprise Carl at all that someone tried to blow up the school. At least now the school board would see how big a mistake they had made.

Carl's world was crumbling bit by rotten bit. He couldn't even sit on his front porch these days, what with the Jacksons coming and going, waving at him and saying hi and expecting a response.

What was he supposed to do? Was he supposed to act like none of this made a difference?

Carl sought solace with a relative who lived not far from the southern edge of Chicago, just across the state line in Gary, Indiana. His cousin, Ralph Bensema, worked in a steel mill, and many of his coworkers were Blacks who had come north to escape the lack of opportunity and outright discrimination of the South. Ralph understood Carl's situation and would listen as Carl shared his anger over all the changes happening around him, especially next door.

Carl trusted Ralph's counsel. Ralph, too, felt that things around him were moving too fast, and that white men were in danger of losing their grip on things because of uppity Blacks who no longer knew their place. Ralph told Carl he had joined a group that would set things right. The Ku Klux Klan, his cousin said, were standing strong, defending what America stood for, and Indiana had long been a proud Klan stronghold. More than that, Ralph had said, the Klan knew how to instill fear and not be pushed around.

"We act in secrecy, see, using surprise," Ralph said. Carl had told Ralph about the beating of George Clement, and Ralph said that the Klan actually operated based on the same principles. "There is no greater motivator than fear," Ralph added. Carl had come out to Gary after work one afternoon and he and Ralph were sitting on lawn chairs in the shade of Ralph's carport.

"But, see," Carl said, "I don't get the whole robes and hoods thing. Why not just let them see who you are?"

"Mystery," said Ralph. "We don't wear the robes all the time, but we do when we want to create fear. If they can't see who you are, they imagine the worst. You and I both know the colored race is inferior. They are subhuman and fearful by nature. Look at how they choose to live, piled on top of each other in slums. More animal than human. See, we just scare the hell out of them, and it doesn't hurt to string one of them up every now and then to remind them who's boss."

"I'm not sure I could go that far," Carl said. He looked out at a couple of kids riding bikes down Ralph's street, and wondered who in the neighborhood knew Ralph was in the Klan.

"Nobody has to do anything they don't want to do," Ralph said. "That's one of the beautiful things about the Klan. We really are a family. We take care of each other and we send messages that need to be sent."

Carl was drinking a bottle of Blatz beer and mindlessly moved the bottle from hand to hand.

"You know that bomb that went off in your kids' school the other night?" Ralph now had Carl's full attention. "I knew all about it before it happened. It wasn't me. See, didn't need to be. We got kindred spirits all over the place, even in high places, like where no one would suspect."

"What d'ya mean 'high places?'" Carl asked, looking around. They were in the carport, sure, but they were more or less outdoors and Carl wasn't sure who might be listening.

"Let's just say this group knows how to be selective about serving and protecting," Ralph said. He spoke loudly and confidently.

Carl was puzzled and spoke in a softer voice. "I don't get it." He thought longer while Ralph sat without saying more. "Wait a minute," Carl said, practically in a whisper. "You don't mean the cops, do you?"

"Look, I trust you to keep your mouth shut about this," Ralph said quietly. "That's all I'm gonna say. But you can't breathe this to a soul. And I'll know if you do."

Carl put the Blatz down and stood up. He needed time to think. He agreed with what Ralph had been saying. He knew in his soul that colored people were inferior. It was kind of a mistake, he thought, even to call them "people." Carl walked to the end of the driveway, looked at the kids on bikes who were up the street by now, and then walked back into the carport.

"Why should the South have all the fun?" Ralph said. "I'd love to have you join the group, if you're strong enough to be part of something like this."

Carl took a couple of deep breaths and Ralph spoke again: "I don't know, see, maybe you just like to bark and complain. Are you all talk and no action?"

"That ain't me," Carl said. "I do stuff." He sat down next to his cousin and picked his beer back up.

"See, if you're a man of action," Ralph said, "I think this could be a good fit. You think it over. Take some time. There's no rush. Just remember, you're angry and we're angry. But we do something about it."

Before Carl left, Ralph gave him some reading material in a weathered old duffel bag. When Carl got back to Green Street, he hid the bag in the garage and made sure Florence and their boys didn't see what he was up to.

That night at dinner, Carl announced he had decided to take up a new hobby, woodworking, and that he was going to take a class with his cousin Ralph in Gary. Later that evening, he called Ralph and told him he was in.

Carl felt like a new man. He sensed purpose in his life, a way to make a difference with people who thought just like he did. He was going to be more than a bystander for the first time in his life.

After Carl attended his first klavern meeting, he told Florence he had a special woodworking project he had started in the garage. It was going to be a surprise for the family, so he didn't want Florence or the boys snooping around. Every night, while Florence and the boys would go out to the porch, Carl would go to the garage.

When he went to Gary, he had a special responsibility as the klavern's newest member. It was his job to place the cross in front of the room as the meeting began. He'd never felt so honored in his life.

Seventeen

Their morning routine rarely varied, even on a Saturday: Magnus and Fenna were up before the children, and Magnus made a cup of coffee and turned on the tea kettle for Fenna while she made the bed. Magnus, dressed in pajamas, a flannel robe, and corduroy slippers no matter the season or weather, shuffled to the front door, stood on the porch, and stretched to the sky to get his circulation going. Only then would he look to find the *Chicago Tribune*. If the paperboy was on target that day, heaving the paper with one hand while juggling his bicycle handlebars with the other, the newspaper would be on the porch at best or the steps at least. On the days of a bad toss, Magnus would find the *Tribune* in the bushes in front of the basement windows.

Magnus found this day's edition on the third step. He yawned as he picked it up and looked up and down the block to see if any other neighbors were up. Carl Bensema was out, and Magnus waved. Carl did not wave back.

Before going inside, Magnus unrolled the paper to read the headline, and what he saw caught his breath. He read the first few paragraphs before he scurried back inside to give Fenna the news. The *Tribune* had broken a major story of corruption, scandalous even by Chicago standards.

"Fenna, have a seat. You're not going to believe this." Magnus shuffled into the kitchen, looking as if he'd seen a ghost on the sidewalk. He set the newspaper on the table for Fenna to read the headline: "The Klan and the Cops."

"The *Trib* says that the Chicago Police Department assigned an officer to go undercover because of rumors that some cops had joined the Ku Klux Klan."

"The what?" Fenna asked.

"You know, the cross burners with the white robes and pointed head things with the eyes cut out." He waved his hands into a point, drawing a picture for Fenna. "The undercover cop uncovered a klavern—one of their groups—that meets in an officer's apartment. A cop was some muckety-muck in the Klan and a policeman at the same time! Do you believe this?"

She looked back at him through sleepy eyes: "Let me get my tea before I try to understand this." After settling back down with her tea bag steeping, she said, "So, I don't get it. Why can't you belong to both?"

Magnus shook his head in disbelief. "Fenna, the Klan is bad business. They hate Jews, Catholics, and especially coloreds. They preach white supremacy, and they act on their hatred. They lynch Negroes and firebomb churches. I mean you hear about this stuff in Alabama and Mississippi, but this is right here in Chicago."

"Magnus, you're worked up. Keep your voice down or you'll wake the kids." She took out her tea bag and twisted it around a spoon.

"Unbelievable." He went back to the article. "It says the apartment had a six-foot tall white cross in a stand between Confederate and United States flags and was full of pamphlets they used for recruiting. One they found asked, '*Who is an American?*'"

Fenna yawned. "Sounds very weird. Why not just join a bowling league? It's a guy thing, right?"

"Fenna, this isn't funny," he said, looking up at his wife. "And, get this—it says that the police department is investigating a possible connection between bombings in Chicago neighborhoods."

"Are you saying ...?" she asked, blowing across the top of her cup of tea.

"That's exactly what I'm saying."

"The Klan bombed our kids' school?" Fenna shivered and drew the collar of her bathrobe tighter.

"Well, it doesn't say. Says the leader is a guy named Tyler Heaton, but no other names have been released." Magnus folded the paper on the kitchen table. Fenna reached over and put her hand on his hands. They sat in silence, letting this suddenly disturbing news sink in.

"This is scary," she said.

"Think about all that has happened this summer."

"That's what I am thinking about," Fenna said. She took a sip of tea and then said, "I'm mostly thinking about one thing that happened."

"Erik riding in the police car?" Magnus said.

"Precisely."

They looked at each other in a moment of shared epiphany and said, "You don't suppose ..."

Before they could say anything else, Erik appeared in front of them in his pajamas and frowsy hair, awakened by the kitchen conversation. "Don't suppose what? You woke me up."

"Me too." Kristen had emerged from her bedroom and entered the kitchen. "It's Saturday, right? We sleep in. What's going on?"

"I heard you say something about my riding in the police car," Erik said. "So, yeah. What's going on?"

Erik and Kristen took their seats at the table and looked at their parents, who looked at each other to see who would start the explanation.

"Your father found something in the newspaper this morning," Fenna said. "He'll explain it to you."

Magnus broke a smile and nodded his head at Fenna, as if to say, "Nicely done. I see what you did there." He gathered his thoughts while filling two bowls with cornflakes and milk and set them before Erik and Kristen. Fenna gave them spoons and stood behind Magnus, now seated, gently rubbing her husband's shoulders.

"Here's what we were talking about." Magnus spoke in a quiet voice to add gravitas to his explanation. "The *Tribune* this morning has a story about Chicago policemen belonging to a secret group of white men who believe that people who are colored or Jewish or even Catholic have no place in America. And sometimes, starting years ago and still today, they will hang people and burn or bomb homes or churches or schools to send a message of hate. And the paper says a group of them are right here in Chicago. That's bad news, really bad news. Even worse, because some of them are policemen."

"I don't understand," Kristen said. "How can the good guys be bad guys at the same time? Sounds like they're really mixed up."

"That's just it," Fenna said. "And it gets more serious because the police have power, and we want to trust them. We want to believe they're out to protect everyone and certainly not harm anyone. That's their job."

"Look," Magnus said. "The paper doesn't say the ones they've discovered have done anything wrong, at least nothing they can find yet. It's now an investigation, so we'll have to wait and see. But they do belong to a secret society called the Ku Klux Klan, which does terrible things."

"Ku Klux Klan? What kind of name is that?" Erik said.

"Don't know how they got the name," Magnus said. "Sometimes they're just called the KKK or the Klan."

"Ok, that's enough about this for now," Fenna said. "Sorry to wake you up. And don't you worry about this stuff. We're safe here. Finish your cereal, and you can go back to bed if you want or catch your Saturday morning cartoons. Either way, let's get the day going."

After he finished his cereal, Erik got dressed and went straight to the *Encyclopedia Americana*. The thirty-volume, leather-bound, gold-embossed treasure filled the top three shelves of the bookcase and was purchased on an installment plan after a visit from a door-to-door salesman. The family had gathered in the front room to hear his pitch and when he assured Magnus and Fenna that a set of encyclopedias "were always on display in the best homes," they were convinced.

When Erik read the entry about the Ku Klux Klan, he thought that the Green Street Boys needed to hear about it. He walked down Green Street and stood on the porches of the others, calling them to come out. Pete and Frank joined him; Eddie, to his frustration, couldn't come out because of his Saturday morning accordion lesson.

"This better be good," Pete said. "I'm missing *Bugs Bunny* for this."

"Yeah, what's the big deal? I was about to go to the library," Frank said.

"Trust me. This is big," Erik replied. "My dad showed us something from the front page of the *Trib*. Something about the Ku Klux Klan and Chicago cops. Somebody went undercover and found out about it. So, ever heard of the Klan? That's what they're called for short."

"You got us over here for that?" Pete said. "Who gives a rip? My dad read that story and said they didn't have anything. I'm outta here."

"I've heard of the Klan," Frank said. "My grandpa tells stories about them, about when he went to Notre Dame."

"Wait, your grandpa went to Notre Dame? Did he play football? Did he know Paul Hornung?" Pete was suddenly engaged.

"Who's Paul Hornung?" Frank said.

"Who's Paul Hornung? Who's Paul Hornung? I don't believe it! What kind of ignoramus are you?" Pete was incensed. "Only the best football player in the whole world. The guy who rips the Bears to shreds every year. Get your head out of your rear!" Pete threw his hands in the air. "I don't believe it!"

"Okay, okay! Cool it, Pete. Back off," Erik said. "Not everybody loves football. Frank said his grandfather went to Notre Dame. Even if he played football, there's no way he played with Paul Hornung. Think about it."

"Do the math, Pete," Frank said. "I said my grandfather. He was there in the 1920s or '30s, something like that."

"So, now do you get it, Pete?" Erik said. "You're unbelievable sometimes, ya know?"

Frank told his grandfather's story. When his grandfather was a student, the Klan planned a march in downtown South Bend. Notre Dame's president told the students to ignore them and stay away. But that just got the students interested and Frank's grandfather was among hundreds—including some football players and several Irish from Chicago—who attacked the Klan during their march. The students took the robes and masks off the Klan members and exposed them as mere mortals. They pushed the Klan into alleys where they beat them up. Some students took potatoes from a barrel in front of a grocery store and threw them through the windows of the Klan headquarters. Notre Dame's quarterback took a potato and made a perfect throw and smashed the cross in one of the windows.

Pete and Erik were mesmerized.

"Well at least it has something to do with football," Pete said. "Can we talk to your grandpa some time?"

"I wish you could," Frank said. "He died last year. My dad says he died of my grandmother's hypochondria. It just wore him out." Frank laughed at the family joke, but Pete and Erik simply sat quietly.

"Maybe we need to band together to fight the Klan," Erik said after a while.

"I don't know," Frank said. "If it's the cops, they have guns."

Later, after Frank and Pete had gone home, Erik sat by himself on the porch, wondering about how some things never change and how hate never seems to die. He thought about Frank's grandfather taking a stand and wondered if he was afraid that day. After a while, he went inside and pulled down another encyclopedia and read about Notre Dame. The incident Frank described didn't appear.

EIGHTEEN

The Schaap family was still adjusting to the second story walk-up apartment across from the Englewood Christian School. They loved the view, the convenience of their new home, and the chance it gave the children to play in the school playground with new friends after school. But walking up and down stairs was never part of their experience in Nigeria. Here, they were up and down the stairs so often that the music of shoes on creaky steps seemed distinctly American to them.

The landlords, Fred and Bernice Bruinius, had seven grandchildren attending the school, and their grocery store was a fixture in the neighborhood. It was one of the mom-and-pop places scattered throughout Englewood, soon to vanish with the coming of supermarket chains featuring, of all things, grocery carts and aisle after aisle of choice. Bruinius's was also the heaven-on-Earth location of penny candy assortments, where students gathered after the dismissal bell each school day.

Fred and Bernice were good landlords, friendly and sincerely interested in the Schaaps' well-being. To show her appreciation, Ruth volunteered to take stock of the store inventory at least once each week. It was stimulating to learn the variety of items in the store and the American way of marketing products. This gave Ruth a chance to meet people in the neighborhood, place names with faces, and meet the parents of some of their children's classmates. Bernice placed two small paper bags filled with cavity-causing goodies in Ruth's hand each time she came in.

On the north side of the building an enclosed stairwell turned to a small landing at the top of the second floor and the entry door to the Schaap apartment. The living room faced the school across the street. Beneath the large picture window in the center of the room sat an overstuffed couch, a Persian rug, a bookcase, and two unmatched upholstered chairs, all donated by Grace Christian Reformed Church members. The handmade Dutch lace curtains adorning the picture window provided a ready reminder of the ethnic community into which the Schaaps were now embedded.

One week after the bomb went off at the Englewood Christian School, just before daybreak, a rock was thrown through the second-story picture window of the Schaap apartment. It shattered the glass, tore through the Dutch lace curtains, and left window fragments lying on the couch and floor. The *Chicago Tribune* front page was wrapped around the rock.

Naomi and Benjamin's bedroom was closest to the living room, and after the crash, Naomi peeked around the corner of the bedroom to see what had happened. "Mama and Baba, come quick! Come see this!"

Benjamin came up alongside her and she said, "Do not move, Benjamin. There is glass on the rug there, by the rock."

Michael and Ruth turned on the living room lights and held their children close to them.

"Who would do such a thing as this?" Naomi asked. "Why is this happening?"

Michael went back to the bedroom for his slippers and then got a dustpan and broom. He unwrapped the newspaper around the rock. It was the front page, the same front page the Pedersens had read, detailing the Klan investigation, but with the words 'Go Home' scribbled across the newsprint in bright red letters. Michael let the paper fall onto the Persian rug.

"What does it say, Baba?" Naomi asked.

Ruth picked up the paper and then shook her head in disgust and disbelief. "Tell them, Michael. Tell them what it says. They need to know."

"Someone who doesn't like us being here wrote some angry words," Michael said. "They want us to go back to Nigeria."

The children sat in their pajamas on the living room chairs across from the couch below the window where the rock landed and watched their parents sweep away the residue of hate from the living room floor. Michael sealed the empty wind-filled space with a blanket and thumbtacks forced into the window trim. All of this was done in silence.

The silence lingered over breakfast until Naomi asked, "Baba, can we go home?" Michael and Ruth looked at each other, and Naomi said, "I think those people with the brick are right. I don't like it here anymore. Even before the brick, I dream. Good dreams of our real home in Nigeria. Bad dreams where I am alone and afraid around here."

Ruth reached out and took Naomi's hand. After looking at her daughter for a moment, she turned to her son and asked, "And how about you Benjamin? How do you feel about being here?"

"What happened this morning scares me," Benjamin said. "I do not know if things will change, really. I read the words on the note." Tears were forming in his eyes. "Have we done something wrong?"

His father spoke: "We—this family—have done nothing wrong. What's wrong is that there are some people who are so full of hate for anyone who is not like them that they do stupid, evil things. I know this is hard to understand, but it's true. But you must believe me and your mother when we say that whoever did this will be punished for destroying this window and for frightening you." He looked intently at Naomi and Benjamin, who were listening but didn't show signs of being convinced. "Listen," he said in a firm yet gentle tone, "it's sad to say, but there's evil all over the world. Both here in Chicago, and in Nigeria. Yet we believe there are stronger forces in this world than hate."

"How do you know these bad people won't do something even worse?" Naomi asked. "The kids at school say there were no troubles before we came."

"Listen, my children," Ruth said. "This is about the color of our skin. That rock did not fly like a bird who lost its way. It came from someone's hand on the strength of a hate-filled heart. It came in the dark to frighten us. To make us want to leave and go home. We will not let them win. We have each other, and we cannot let small minds and hateful hearts be stronger than love."

"I feel okay when I am with you," Naomi said, "but it is frightening to go to school. Can we just stay home and not go to school anymore?"

Ruth touched Naomi's face and gently stroked her cheek. "Whenever I am afraid, it helps me to remember that there is something good behind my fear. When I am afraid of the dark, it is because I love the light. When I am afraid of harm, I know it is because I love life and freedom. When I fear for your safety, it is because you are a gift to us and the world." The children relaxed as she spoke. She moved her hand from Naomi and put it on top of Benjamin's hand. "Benjamin and Naomi, I am so sorry you've been frightened. Your world should be filled with freedom and joy. These hate-filled people need to climb a tree, ride a bike, or count the stars. Remember that Jesus said that all must be like children to enter his kingdom—children who are not afraid and live carefree with their dreams. We have journeyed a long way from home and this has not been a good start here. You are right about that. But I believe there will be better days ahead."

They sat in silence for a few more moments, staring at the patched window space and looking down at the carpet for missing pieces of glass. The sound of footsteps on the stairwell called them out of their thoughts, and a knock at the door brought them to stand back together. Michael opened the door to find Sergeant Mick O'Rourke at the top of the stairs, out of breath from the climb.

"Good morning. Mr. Schaap. Or is it Reverend Schaap?" O'Rourke asked.

"It's Mr. Schaap," Michael said. "But how did you know my name?"

"It's our business to know names," O'Rourke said between breaths with a tap on Schaap's shoulder and a quick laugh. "Look, we got word of an incident here this morning. That right?"

"Yes, that's right. Just before daybreak. A rock through the window there, with newspaper and a note wrapped around it. I was just about to call the police."

"No need," O'Rourke said as he moved past Michael into the apartment and looked at the spot where the blanket had been tacked over the broken window. "Just got word about it. Look, it's gotta be tough for you, bein' a mixed-race family and all. Don't see that around here very often, that's for sure. But, no one hurt, I hope?" O'Rourke looked past Michael at Ruth, Benjamin, and Naomi. "You kids all right? Put some shoes on when you walk around in here or you'll get glass in your feet."

The children looked at the large uniformed man and Naomi surprised herself by speaking, "Can you find who did this?"

"Well, where's the rock? Let me see it. And the note. I'll take it, it's evidence. And I'll make a report. Anything else I can do for you while I'm here?"

"Can you give me a note so that I do not have to go to school?" Naomi said.

O'Rourke laughed and said, "I wish I could, young lady. But then I might get called into the principal's office. You go to school across the street, right?"

Before Naomi could answer, Ruth took a step forward and said, "And how do you know that, may I ask?"

"Well, missus, you can just chalk that up to good police work," O'Rourke replied. And with a tip of his hat he smiled, opened the door to leave, and said, "You know, bein' mixed race and all, I'd be extra careful around here. Some folks don't take to that too good. And I noticed the door wasn't locked downstairs. You should do that from now on. Things like rocks through the window? Probably just tryin' to frighten you. But, you never know." He started to leave and then said, "Mr. Schaap, can I have a word with you in the hall?"

Once in the hall, O'Rourke turned to Michael and said, "You should take that note seriously."

"I take it very seriously," Michael said.

"You should," O'Rourke said. "Beautiful family. It would be a pity to see them harmed. 'Go Home' is good advice. Africa is the best place for them. With their own kind." With that, O'Rourke lumbered slowly down the stairs. Benjamin and Naomi ran to a side window to watch him squeeze into the driver's seat of his police car.

"We serve and protect," Benjamin said, reading the words on the side of the car.

Michael came in from the hall, and he and Ruth stared at each other for a moment.

"I do not like it that he knows so much about us," Ruth said.

"Me neither," her husband said.

A few days later, the city approved the repairs to the Englewood Christian School building, gave the school permission to reopen, and Naomi and Benjamin returned to their classes. In the days and weeks after the brick landed among glass shards on their couch and living room floor, the Schaaps received anonymous letters with similar messages. Yet, as word spread through the school and church community of the threats and harassment, they also received phone calls and letters expressing love and concern, encouraging them to remember that God watches over their family as he does the sparrows of the field.

Among the notes they received was this:

> Dear Ruth,
>
> I am so sorry to hear about what happened to you and your dear loved ones. I can't imagine the evil that might possess someone to send hate through your window like that. I know God will forgive them, but it would take me some time, that's for sure. Magnus and our children send their love. We want you to know we are glad you are here. Your presence, your witness, is inspiring to us and many others. We need you and your family here.
>
> May God's Peace Rest Upon You,
>
> Fenna Pedersen

With every letter of encouragement and every scribbled note, the Schaaps felt less alone in this strange and divided community. Still, sleep did not come easy for any of them.

Nineteen

The bombing of the Englewood Christian School and subsequent closing for repairs gave the school year an uncertain start. The board still had to deal with the postponed motion to start a property search committee, and, as they headed to their October meeting, concerns about the curriculum and orthodoxy of teachers took a back seat. The board's immediate concern was finding their way through the changes around them. So much seemed beyond their control.

Board Chair Sam Slager called the meeting to order and offered a prayer to make sure things got off on the right foot. Slager had learned the art of public prayer by not just absorbing the Thees and Thous of the King James Bible but also by listening to the cadences of the Reverend Calvin Wolthuis and other Christian Reformed dominees over the years.

> Our Father in Heaven, we call upon Thee in the evening hour of this day to be in our midst as we deliberate and discuss matters of importance to Thee and Thy Kingdom. It behooves us to seek Thy

> face in times of blessing and times of struggle. We beseech Thee that Thou wilt be pleased in Thine infinite mercy to graciously look upon Thy children here at our school that they, daily following Jesus, may joyfully cleave unto him in true faith, firm hope, and ardent love. We pray in the name of our Lord Jesus Christ, who with Thee and the Holy Spirit, one only God, lives and reigns forever. Amen.

With such verbal dexterity, Slager had once entertained the idea of attending seminary and becoming a minister himself, and had been encouraged by his parents and teachers to consider this his calling in life. It turned out instead that he loved the idea of operating his own business. He was his own boss, made a comfortable living, and found selling shoes a holiness unto itself when done for the glory of God.

Tonight's meeting would demand its own eloquence and careful thought. Slager started the meeting by asking Principal Rodney Hoekema to remind the board of all that had transpired since the last meeting. A stillness settled over the band room, where new windows and fresh masonry work stood as reminders of that awful, chilling night of the bombing.

The principal's summary brought them to the business at hand. Slager was careful not to tip his hand on the motion to create a property search committee. He showed a sanctified poker face so that an open, unbiased conversation could take place. Arie Vos, the oldest board member, and the one who had postponed the motion a month earlier, took the initiative. Vos was generally regarded by the younger men as "walking wisdom," and reminded them of the reason for his parliamentary maneuver the previous month. "Those who founded this school," he said, rising to face his fellow board members, "the generation before me and you, worked hard and sacrificed the comforts of life for the sake of providing a Christian school to stand with the home and the church in raising children in the faith. They, like all of us, took their covenant vows, made at baptism, seriously and wholeheartedly. You know this. We are forever indebted to them. Never in their wildest dreams would they have considered moving this school out of Englewood." He paused and took a deep breath. "But I've thought long and hard about this. We do need to talk about this. Think about this. Pray about this. Last month I moved to postpone this motion to give us time. I thought seriously about coming tonight and moving to table the motion indefinitely. But as I have thought and prayed about this, I don't think we should do that. I will not stand in the way of an open conversation about the location of our school." After a moment, he sat.

There was silence as the board members looked around to see who would speak. Finally, Mel Lamsma cleared his throat and said, "Well, for starters, in the real estate world, two churches from different denominations on the east side of Halsted have already sold and they're moving southwest of the city." Several heads nodded in confirmation.

Hannes Piersma, who had raised the idea of relocating to the board a month earlier, said, "Look, I know for sure that since we last met two houses sold on my block, and, just like that, we have two colored families down the street."

"The handwriting is on the wall," Henk Koning said. "We might as well wake up and smell the coffee."

"May I please remind all of us that we should speak for or against the motion," Sam Slager said.

"I thought I did, Sam," Henk Koning said. "Let me make it real plain. I'm talking about the motion, and I'm in favor of appointing a property search committee. That good enough?" He didn't look directly at Slager but made a face of exasperation that he showed to the other board members.

"Yes, that's good enough. Thank you," Slager said.

There was another pause, and the room grew quiet enough that the sound of seconds ticking by on the new band room clock could be heard.

"I really don't know if I'm speaking for or against the motion, so bear with me," Meine Decker said, leaning forward as he spoke. "I think I can share this, but I won't mention the name. I talked to someone this week and his perspective might be helpful. He said Englewood, not just our little part of it, is at a turning point. We love it here. We'd all say that, I think. And the Negroes who are moving in love it, too. It's all about community. Could we learn to live together? Is that even possible? Since we both, Negro and white, love this area, the shopping district, the transportation, Hamilton Park, being close enough to downtown—you get what I'm saying—why do we whites think we have to move somewhere? Doesn't make much sense to me. There are two Catholic parishes, and by my count, over twenty Protestant churches. What happens if we all leave?" He left the question hanging for an uncomfortable moment. "So, I guess I'm speaking against the motion. We appoint a committee, then it's all over. No more questions. It's a done deal the moment that news gets out. It's not a question of where we end up. It's a question of how soon we move."

"Meine," Mel Lamsma said, "I've always respected you and the way you think. I truly do. But I think you're dreaming. Show me where Blacks and whites living together ever worked in Chicago. I'd like to know of one example. And not just Chicago. Coloreds and whites just don't get along together. Anywhere. And here's the truth: Shady realtors are making a killing these days. They even have a name for it: 'block busting.' They find a way to settle a Negro family on an all-white street and then put out the word that whites will lose money—big money—if they don't move quickly. They're fear mongers. Some of them hire colored teenagers to walk through white neighborhoods, just to make their presence known. They want us to move because they'll buy our homes for a steal and turn around and sell them at a high price to the Blacks. So, guess who wins? They do! They always do. And Blacks and whites alike are the poorer for it. That's what's going on here. We can't make coloreds and whites like each other, but we can make sure we don't get swindled." He looked around the room and saw heads nodding yes.

The elephant in the room had just plopped its enormous derrière in the center: Race relations in Chicago always found its way into conversations, decisions, imaginations, and actions. It was the stuff of sports, politics, playgrounds, parks, and shifting neighborhoods. Race was all over Chicago, in big ways and small. Whose streets were plowed in the winter and whose were the last to be cleared? Who got the new grocery stores and who didn't? Circling around all of this for white Chicago was fear. Fear for physical safety. Fear of declining property values. Fear of being among the last whites on the block. Fear of the unknown.

The board sat in silence until Principal Rodney Hoekema offered a way out. "I think we might be missing something," he said. The board members looked at him eagerly. "We haven't talked about enrollment. Our numbers have been strong, but let's face it, if everyone moves, our enrollment will sink faster than a stone in the ocean." Several of the board members nodded in affirmation of the principal's concern. Enrollment was an issue they all could get behind. Even if it was not an issue at the moment, which it was not, the board felt it would be wise to act in anticipation of a dreary future. No one wanted to sound uncaring and callous on race, but they all had a responsibility for the health of the school. The fear of a future enrollment decline carried the day.

The discussion on the motion continued for another half-hour with several members sharing in the newfound concern about enrollment. Finally, Sam Slager pointed out what everyone sensed: everything to be said on the matter had been said. He called the question, and the vote to establish a property search committee passed by a unanimous vote, except for Meine Decker, who asked that his negative vote be placed in the minutes. Sam Slager asked Mel Lamsma and Principal Hoekema if they would work with him to put a property search team together. Henk Koning immediately volunteered to be on the search team.

With nothing else on the agenda, Sam Slager called for the adjournment of the meeting and asked if there was a volunteer to close the gathering in prayer. The room fell silent, no one looking up from the table, each waiting for someone else to step up. Usually, Principal Rodney Hoekema could be counted on in a moment like this, but he, too, was silent. Slager, despite his reputation for florid prayers, couldn't think of a thing to say. After an uncomfortable, hushed minute and sensing nothing would happen unless he did something, Slager said, "Pray with me. Our Father who art in Heaven, hallowed be Thy name. Thy Kingdom come, Thy will be done ..."

It was only a few weeks later that the board called a special meeting of the Englewood Christian School Association. The board had been busy. They had found property for a new school in the southwest suburb of Oak Lawn, a community already populated with families who had moved from Englewood. In addition, they had found a willing buyer for the existing building: the Chicago Public Schools. The meeting was held in the Grace Christian Reformed Church, and the church was filled to the balcony. The recommendation was approved by a resounding voice vote. The few negative voices quickly disappeared below the churning chatter assuring the future move.

At the conclusion of the meeting, a letter was read, which would be sent to the school's constituents the following day, stating the reasons for the move and announcing the good news of the pending sale of the school.

> At last night's Association meeting the decision was made, with a resounding majority of votes from within the Association, to close our school at its current location, largely because of declining enrollment, given the steady move of our Association members from Englewood. We are pleased to not only announce that we have secured expansive property in the suburb of Oak Lawn, but also give thanks that the Chicago Board of Education has offered us $110,000 for our current building, which they hope to occupy next fall. We have accepted their offer. Our current building will now be used to educate children of our neighborhood to whom God has given a different color of skin. We pray that in the future God may provide a way so that we may be able to witness to these people the wonderful grace of God as revealed in Christ. In the meantime, let us harbor no bitterness or resentment. If we do, we can no longer sing, 'Red and yellow, black and white, they are precious in His sight,' a song which has echoed often from the halls of our classrooms.

At the association meeting, Magnus and Fenna were two of those who meekly voiced their votes against the sale. As they walked away, Fenna said, "I don't understand. We have declining enrollment, yet the city can't wait to buy our school building because they have students ready to fill the building. It doesn't add up."

"It does when you understand what's really going on," her husband said quietly, with the sound of their footsteps being the only noise they heard as they walked home.

Twenty

When Willowby Jackson suggested it would be nice to visit with the Pedersens again, his wife Sheila said, "Do you really think I have time for this?" She reminded him that she worked for a living while he sat in his office dreaming up his next sermon and writing notes on a skinny scrap of paper whenever an idea struck him, knowing full well that he'd wing it the coming Sunday just like he always did and preach as the Spirit led him. "Do you forget," she said, "that I steer nearly 175 students in five sections every day, freshmen to seniors, eighty percent of whom are bored into a comatose state while I try to inspire them to greater heights in English literature?" He started to say something but could see she wasn't finished. "And then, Reverend Doctor Jackson, I come home and grade papers and read essays and plan my next day's work while you stare longingly across the street wanting to make nice with the white folks who live there."

But Willowby was persuasive: not only did he convince Sheila that they should try again with their neighbors, but when he crossed the street and mentioned wanting to get together again to the Pedersens, Fenna invited them over for coffee that Friday evening.

A few days later, they were together, and the start of the weekend meant the adults were dressed more casually: Willowby was not wearing his clerical collar or a suit but a knit shirt and dark pants. Sheila looked to Kristen and Erik like someone who might be on *American Bandstand*, appearing younger than her age in tight slacks and a light sweater and looking like no teacher they'd ever encountered at Englewood Christian. Fenna had changed from her housedress and apron to a skirt and colorful blouse, and Magnus had taken off his suit as soon as he reached home and looked relaxed in his casual slacks, plaid shirt, and tasseled loafers.

The Jacksons sat on the living room couch next to the television with the big rabbit ears antenna. Magnus and Fenna sat in matching easy chairs in front of the windows with their backs to Green Street and the Jacksons' home. Kristen sat on the floor at Fenna's feet and Erik did the same in front of Magnus. In addition to the coffee and cookies on the coffee table, Kristen and Erik were each given a bottle of Pepsi, a treat usually reserved for holidays and birthdays, marking tonight as a special occasion. They had been encouraged by their parents to be very good listeners and polite hosts, and their parents had invited them to join in the conversation if they felt like it.

After a few initial pleasantries, Willowby cleared his throat and spoke: "Sheila and I want you to know we realize how unusual—maybe even risky—it is for you to welcome us into your home. You're the only ones on this block to do so."

After both Magnus and Fenna mentioned something about it being the neighborly thing to do, Willowby continued, "Here's where I think this could take us, all six of us." With a warm smile, Willowby looked directly at Erik and then Kristen. "Some place rare, frankly. Almost like traveling to a foreign country, given the state of things around our country and here in Chicago." He paused and then said, "I have some thoughts on how we can build on this good start, if you're willing to hear me out."

Fenna and Magnus looked at each other and the children turned around to see how their parents would respond. Magnus said, "We're willing to give anything a try. I guess we're game, right, Fenna?" She smiled and nodded. Erik took a gulp of his Pepsi and tried his hardest not to burp.

"I want to talk about what it would take for us to really be friends," Willowby said, sitting up and clasping his hands together. He then spoke from his heart about not just acknowledging what they had in common but talking openly and freely about how they differed from each other. "Where we differ," Willowby said, "especially in our struggles—that's the hard part. We need to do our best listening here." He looked at both Magnus and Fenna, who were focused and intent: "What we have in common—our humanity, our faith—that's one thing. But what's different beyond our skin color is significant. I'm talking about our histories and our culture."

"And please don't ever say you're colorblind," Sheila said. "We hear that a lot, and honestly, it's disrespectful. If you're blind to my color, then you don't really see me. Same with us toward you."

Magnus shifted in his seat and Erik and Kristen focused on their Pepsi bottles. "We appreciate your frankness," Magnus said, "and I for one just learned something." Erik and Kristen looked up at him. "I agree it's rare for this kind of thing to happen, where we sit down and talk, listen to each other, make a start at friendship." Magnus put his hand onto Erik and gently steered him aside and then stood up. He turned toward the picture window for a moment and looked out across Green Street before turning and facing Willowby and Sheila on the couch. "But look," he said, "there's something you need to know. Our reality is that our school board just took a big step. They appointed a property search committee to relocate to the southwest suburbs. They moved very quickly and actually bought land in Oak Lawn and have sold the school building to the Chicago Board of Education." He searched Willowby and Sheila's faces. "Seems like this has happened overnight, and to us, at least, is a bit premature. And now the rumor is that our church will do the same thing. It all looks like leaving is a foregone conclusion."

Willowby said, "I'm sorry to hear that." Sheila turned and looked hard at her husband.

Magnus returned to his seat and said, "People—our friends and church members—are moving out of Englewood. It's starting to feel like a tidal wave, out of control. And as much as we'd like to stay, we want to be near our church and school, wherever they end up. I guess that's most important to us."

Kristen and Erik looked at each other, wide-eyed.

"I appreciate your honesty," Sheila said. "Seems to be a pattern wherever you look in Chicago. Blacks move in. Whites move out. But you haven't told us why. That's what I'm curious about." She paused and tried to smile. Her voice caught as she said, "What is it about us Black folks that makes you white people want to move? If you won't live near us, won't get to know us and give us a chance to know you, you won't ever stand with us."

Willowby inched forward on the couch. He was starting to say, "Now Sheila—" when he was interrupted by Kristen.

"But I don't want to move," she said.

"Kristen. Erik," Fenna said. "To be honest, we've only started to think about it. Maybe we should have told you, but we haven't decided anything for sure yet."

"I don't want to move either," Erik said. "All my friends live here."

"Sounds like a big surprise for you kids," Willowby said, "but Sheila and I aren't surprised. It would be a big surprise to hear you say you wouldn't move." He took a cookie off the coffee table and looked at his hosts.

"You can see it's important for us to be near our church and children's school, can't you?" Magnus asked.

"Sure," Sheila said. "But let me ask you something. My feeling is that fear is in the driver's seat. Am I right? Fear of all things Black?"

"I'm not afraid," Erik said, turning to all the adults. "I'm not. Are you, Kristen?" Kristen nodded her assent. "Mom and Dad, are you afraid?"

Magnus looked to Fenna, who folded her arms across her chest. A reality was settling over the living room like a lingering, low-lying fog.

"I don't know if I can express what it was like to see our neighbor George Clement in the alley behind our house after he was beaten," Fenna said, unfolding her arms. "I don't have words for my feelings but they are hard to shake." She stopped to gain her composure and then said, "I'm worried about Erik and Kristen's safety. I am sorry, but the suburbs look safer."

Sheila was about to say something when Magnus spoke about the murder of their milkman. "For a lot of us," he said, "that was the last straw. I know crime has happened here before and I know crime happens in the suburbs. But look—I don't know how to say this delicately, but for our friends, Negro crime is worse than white crime." He looked down at the carpet when Sheila spoke.

"Has anyone been arrested in that case?"

Magnus was still looking at the floor while he shook his head no.

"You do realize," Willowby said, "that some of this hysteria is the work of realtors looking to make a quick buck. Have you heard about that?"

"I don't know about real estate agents," Magnus said, looking up at Willowby. "But property values are all anyone seems to talk about after church. They can't wait to compare notes and sound the alarm. The fear is that if you're the last to move out you lose the most value on your home. Fenna and I can't afford to have that happen."

"In many cases a realtor will buy the property and sell it at a large profit," Willowby said. "Whites get ripped off, and when Negroes move in, they get ripped off too. The only ones who come out ahead are the realtors. Any chance to live together goes down the drain."

The group sat in silence, deep in thought. It was quiet enough that they could hear the traffic on Halsted and the barking of a dog down the block. After a while, Sheila said that she appreciated the Pedersens' hospitality and honesty. "You know," she said, "It doesn't have to be this way. You are people of faith, just like we are, and I guess I want to ask you if this is about fear—or faith? Which is stronger, or should be?"

No one answered and they sat in silence until Sheila spoke again: "All this fuss seems to be about borders and geography, distance, or proximity, money, and hate. And plain old ugly racism. Remember, before long fear turns to hate. Fear and hate combine to say, 'Don't get too close, physically, or emotionally.' Since when has distance ever worked out well?"

Again there was silence, and she spoke a third time: "And Erik and Kristen, I'm talking to you, too. I hope you remember this conversation. When you're older and things are the same—which they probably will be—do something about it. Our generation can't figure this out. Maybe yours will." They nodded. Erik had finished his Pepsi and Kristen took a large drink to finish hers.

Willowby said, "Listen, neighbors, we live with fear, too. Why do you think we have guys from our church sit on our front porch every night?" Saying those words eased some of the tension in the room. Fenna looked at her neighbor and nodded. Willowby smiled and said, "Sheila's been spat on walking to the Halsted bus. There's a lot of hate in this neighborhood. We're hated for no other reason than we're Black."

"I'm sorry," Magnus said, looking first at Sheila and then Willowby.

"I am too," Fenna added, also looking at them.

"My hope is that Erik and Kristen will learn from this and do better than our generation," Willowby said. With that, Willowby rose, and then everyone stood as if nothing more could or should be said. Sheila and Willowby extended their hands to Magnus and Fenna and then to Erik and Kristen.

"I don't know what we're going to do," Magnus said. "If we move, maybe we'll regret it. But I just don't see how we can make a difference."

"Well, we'd be sorry to see you go, if that's your decision," Willowby said. "We have a chance to make it together, I really believe that. It's hard to live with the 'what ifs.'"

They all moved slowly through the door and crowded onto the front porch, and before the Jacksons walked down the stairs toward home, they saw Florence and Carl Bensema sitting in the dark on their porch. It was the first time they'd been on their porch together in weeks. Carl's hands were heavily wrapped in bandages, resting on his lap.

Willowby and Sheila walked slowly across the street, waved at Carl and Florence as they drew close, and absorbed being ignored by Carl yet again. Once at their house, Sheila went inside while Willowby turned and waved to the Pedersens, who waved back. Willowby breathed in the still autumn air and saw Michael and Gabriel, their guardian angels, sitting in a parked car in front of the house. Willowby had been so lost in thought as he crossed the street he hadn't noticed them. He looked across the street one more time, wondering if he'd ever have a meaningful conversation with the Pedersens again, wondering if Green Street was destined to be a border instead of a bridge.

Twenty-One

The Green Street Boys gathered on the Pedersen porch the next afternoon. Unless called into a special session, Frank, Pete, and Eddie would wander over to Erik's house after lunch on Saturdays during the school year. As they settled in, the question of what to talk about was on their minds. The White Sox had finished in fifth place, so there wasn't much to talk about there, and though the football season was barely a month old, no one believed the Bears could unseat the Packers. They moaned for a while about schoolwork, and then Frank asked if anyone's family was going to move.

"My parents talked about it last night," Erik said. "It just kind of came up in front of the Jacksons. My parents never even talked to me or my sister about it. The Jacksons found out about it at the same time we did."

"Geez," Pete said.

"Yeah," Erik said. "I don't want to move." Pete, Eddie, and Frank could see Erik was upset.

"Are you mad?" Frank said.

Pete punched Frank in the arm and said, "Well duh, Frank, of course he's mad."

"You don't have to punch me about it," Frank said, twisting his arm in pain.

"Don't be a girl all the time, then," Pete said.

"It's okay," Erik said. "But yeah, it pisses me off." He looked up at the others. "What about you guys? Your parents thinking about it?"

"I don't know, but my aunt and uncle have their place up for sale," Pete said.

Eddie said, "Me and my brother snuck out of bed and sat at the top of the stairs the other night and heard our folks say something about a search party scouting out land for our school. They said if that happens, the church won't be far behind."

"A search party? Scouting?" Frank said. "It sounds like *Gunsmoke*."

Pete punched him in the arm again, and Frank said, "Cut it out," and drew his arm in a circle, trying to work out the pain. "Stop hitting me."

"Well, don't be so stupid," Pete said.

"So what about you, Frank?" Eddie said, ignoring Pete and Frank's fight. "Is your church leaving? Or do you want to stay here with the coloreds? I bet you'll move too, church and school together ... just like us."

"My parents say the church and school will never move," Frank said. "My parents say our family might move, but there is no way the church would move. The Pope won't allow it."

Pete made a fist again but stopped himself. Instead, he spoke: "Some old guy in Rome, who doesn't know crap about Chicago, can tell you not to move?"

"The Pope says that the altar belongs to God and nobody can move it. It stays put."

"That's ridiculous!" Pete said.

"The Pope doesn't make mistakes," Frank said. "There is a word for that ... I think it's pontificate. The Pope does that, and he's always right." Pete swung again but this time Frank was anticipating it and ducked out of the way. "Look, I don't make the rules," Frank said. "Ever since Jesus put Peter on the throne in Rome that's how it works. Peter laid down the law like Jesus wanted it, which says the Pope is in charge of every Catholic church."

"Geez," Pete said. "What a system. The Pope decides everything. He even tells the priests not to get married. If some old Pope ever told me I couldn't get married, I'd tell him to take a flying leap. I don't care how much of a boss he thinks he is."

As Pete was saying that, Kristen Pedersen was walking up the sidewalk, coming home from a friend's house. She heard enough to say, "Who'd want to marry you anyway?" as she walked into the house.

Erik, Eddie, and especially Frank, who was still rubbing his arm, hooted at Pete.

"I'm going to marry Priscilla De Haan," Pete said to the closed door.

"Because she gives you a boner," Frank said. "We've heard that too many times." Frank jumped off the porch into the front yard before Pete had another chance to swing at him.

"Forget the Pope and Priscilla De Haan," Eddie said. "Let's get back to business."

"How can I forget Priscilla De Haan?" Pete said.

"Just like I can't forget Annette Funicello," Frank said. "She's a full-grown woman and all the rest of the Mouseketeers are little kids." Frank came back onto the porch.

"Except for Roy and Jimmie," Erik said.

"I wish I was Cubby," Frank said.

"That's kid stuff," Pete said.

"Annette ain't no kid," Frank said. "She's all woman. And she's all mine."

Eddie turned toward Frank. "I'm serious," Eddie said. "Don't you guys see it? My parents, and Pete and Erik's parents, think the church is us and people like us, so if we move, our church has to move. But the Catholics think the church is for the neighborhood, no matter who lives here."

"The Catholics are better," Frank said, punching Pete in the arm as he spoke.

Pete started to retaliate, but Erik held up his hand and said, "Pete, he owed you that."

They sat in silence. It was one of those October days that couldn't make up its mind, the sun and clouds kept changing places, and a breeze kept blowing leaves across the yard. After a while Eddie looked at Erik and said, "Did your parents say where you're going to move to?" Erik shook his head and shrugged his shoulders. Eddie spoke again, "I mean, what are the chances our parents move onto the same street again?"

They were quiet for a while longer until Eddie said, "The other night, when I was supposed to be sleeping, my parents talked about Roseland and some other place like Evergreen Park, something like that. I guess there are Christian schools there. And churches like ours. And no coloreds. My parents say no coloreds will ever move there."

Pete, still smarting from being punched in the arm, stood up and took a step in Frank's direction, and Frank jumped off the porch again. "Francis A. Sissy," Pete said. "What a little girl." Pete turned toward the others and said, "I don't hear my parents talk about it much. Just about my aunt and uncle. I don't know what's going to happen."

Frank came back to the porch, and once again they sat in silence. A future was taking shape for all of them. Life as they knew it, life as they loved it, wasn't going to be the same. The reason for the seismic shift traced back to the stark reality of Black people moving in and white people moving away.

"So, it sounds like it's the same for all of us," Erik said.

They sat together, chins resting on their knees or backs reclining against the bricks, deep in thought about the implications of moving from their neighborhood to some unknown, never-before-seen destination.

They heard it before they saw it. The low rumble of a diesel engine rounded the corner from 73rd Street and onto Green Street heading north. The truck passed them on the porch and came to a stop in front of Old Man Finnegan's house. The man on the passenger side stepped out, clipboard in hand, cigar clenched between his lips, and climbed the stairs. His girth spilled over his belt, and he looked like he could hug a refrigerator and carry it to the truck with one hand tied behind his back. He didn't have to knock or ring the doorbell—Old Man Finnegan was waiting for him. While there had been no For Sale sign on his lawn, it was plain to see what was happening. The sides of the red truck spelled out in white lettering: "EZ Come, EZ Go! Chicago's Moving Experience."

The Green Street Boys gathered on the sidewalk near Old Man Finnegan's house, overcome by curiosity, temporarily unafraid of the fabled shotgun just inside the door. They saw the old man standing in the doorway with peeling paint all over the door jamb, wrinkled like his skin. He told the mover to bring the truck around back, to park in the alley, so cars could pass each other on narrow Green Street. As the mover walked back to the truck, Old Man Finnegan stepped out on his porch and waved for the Green Street Boys to come closer. They saw no shotgun, so they inched ever so slowly to the steps and much closer to each other, still fearful but nosy enough to approach. They stopped short of the steps—in case they needed to make a run for it—and Frank made sure he stood at the back of the huddle. Then they heard words they would never forget.

"Listen up, you punks," Old Man Finnegan shouted at them. "I'm leaving this place for good." He swept his arms as if to brush the street away. "The neighborhood is going to the dogs." Old Man Finnegan grabbed the wooden porch railing in front of his house, looked down, and pointed to the ground. "So, I guess you'll have to find another place to take a whiz." He slapped his thigh, leaned back with a deep laugh, and waved as he walked back inside and closed the door.

Dumbfounded, Erik, Pete, Eddie, and Frank looked at each other and then at the sidewalk. Erik was the first to speak: "I don't believe it."

"I know one thing for sure," Frank said. "I'm not sneaking up the stairs to see if there really is a shotgun!"

The Green Street Boys decided to end their meeting and go on their way. Erik was eager to tell his parents that Old Man Finnegan was moving.

As he took a few steps back toward his house, Erik turned to watch Frank cross the street and Eddie and Pete head north up the sidewalk. He had a sense that this might be exactly how the future would happen, with his friends slowly slipping away.

Twenty-Two

"Michael and Gabriel," the Jacksons' guardian angels, were a team of men from the Greater Freedom Methodist Church. When the men heard that Sheila called them Michael and Gabriel they liked it and the name stuck. Otis Graves and Marvin Brown were the latest recruits to the Michael and Gabriel team, eager to be the eyes and ears for Willowby and Sheila, ensuring restful nights for their pastor and the first lady of their church.

The routine was simple: Whoever was on that night would typically sit in a parked car in front of the Jackson home until sundown, then move to the Jackson porch and assume their positions until 1 or 2 a.m. Periodically, they took turns walking the gangway between the Jackson home and the Bensema home, scanning the alley and backyard, and returning to the porch.

Most nights were uneventful. Occasionally, someone would stumble out of Donegan's Tavern and shuffle by the house, and it wasn't unusual on Friday or Saturday night for white teenage boys to drive slowly past with their car windows rolled down, shout obscenities and racial slurs, and then speed up and squeal around the corner as soon as they passed the Jackson house.

Who could say what other mayhem might have happened without the presence of a Gabriel and Michael on Green Street?

The very first night on duty for Otis and Marvin proved eventful. The crew had told them about Carl Bensema, whom they called "Catatonic Carl" for his vacant, distant stares. Just before midnight, as Otis was doing the backyard and alley patrol, he saw a light on inside the Bensema garage, shining through a side door window. Otis crouched behind the bushes along the chain link fence and slowly moved closer to the garage to check it out. Through a side window he saw a man on the other side of a parked car standing in front of a workbench with a light hanging from the ceiling above him. That had to be Catatonic Carl. Otis could see his hands were bandaged and he was holding something in the air, looking closely at it.

Otis crept quickly to the porch and whispered for Marvin to join him. They moved quietly back down the gangway, crouching behind the bushes.

"What's that crazy fool doing this time of night?" Marvin said.

"Can't say for sure, but that's some kind of workbench," Otis said. "Look behind him, there's a pegboard with all the tools hanging."

"Who works in a garage this late?" Marvin said. "His old lady must have kicked him out!"

Otis smiled and said, "Don't make me start laughing. This is some weird stuff." After a minute he said, "What you think he's working on?"

Marvin was taller than Otis and had a better view. "Looks to me like he's pouring something into a pipe. Like some plumbing work, I guess."

"Plumbing? I don't know any plumbing that calls for filling a pipe." They watched for a while longer until Otis grabbed Marvin's arm and led him back to the Jacksons' porch. "You thinking what I'm thinking?"

They both nodded together. "That crazy fool is making a bomb!" Marvin scurried into the house and woke Willowby and Sheila, who both threw on robes. Marvin was breathless as he explained their suspicion that Carl was making a pipe bomb. Willowby put his arm around Sheila, who looked very troubled and said, "We need to call the police."

"Are you sure of what you saw?" Willowby said. "I don't know how the police will react if this is a false alarm." He looked at Marvin and then at Sheila, and after taking in her face, Willowby went to the phone in the kitchen and asked Marvin if he wanted to make the call.

"You better do it," Marvin said. "You sound more white than me."

After making the call, Willowby and Sheila watched from the kitchen window with all the lights in the house turned off while Marvin went back to the porch and made Otis laugh by describing Willowby and Sheila's matching bathrobes. They then sat on the porch waiting. All four were praying.

Sergeant Mick O'Rourke was working the night shift and the call was given to him. When he saw the address was 7256 Green Street, he knew it was on the same end of the block as the Pedersens and tried to picture which house it was. He took the unusual step of asking someone to go with him—bombs were outside his comfort zone—and chose Connor McManus, a second-year officer, young, but with a good reputation. They were on the scene within ten minutes.

With the sound of the squad car approaching in the alley, Otis and Marvin slipped back into the bushes alongside the Jacksons' house. This was Otis and Marvin's first night of protection duty and they didn't want it to be their last night on Earth—they feared the cops would shoot first and ask questions later if they saw a couple of young Black men outside at this time of night. Yet they couldn't resist staying outside to see for themselves what happened.

Carl heard the car in the alley and quickly slipped the pipe into a drawer of the workbench and turned off the light hanging above the bench. He thought about making sure the garage door was locked, but didn't feel he had time. He crouched behind his car and waited.

Mick and Connor were approaching the garage when they saw the light go out. They took positions on either side of the door, weapons drawn and raised.

"Whoever's in there, come out with your hands up! This is the police. Don't make us come in. We know you're in there," Mick barked. Connor wiped his sweaty hand on his pant leg.

Carl thought for a moment, then stood, turned the garage light on, and opened the door, stepping out with his bandaged hands in the air. "What's this about?" he said. "Just working on my car here."

Mick and Connor holstered their guns, and Carl breathed easier. "You live here?" Connor asked. "What's your license plate number?" Carl answered with the right number and Connor asked, "What's the emergency with your car that's got you working on it this time of night?"

"Nothing big really. Just couldn't sleep and wanted to check on some things," Carl said.

"What's your name and what's the address?" Mick asked.

"Carl Bensema, 7256 Green Street. I live here with my wife and two boys."

"Don't suppose you have any ID on you, that right?" McManus said.

"No, officer, I don't. Just got out of bed and threw some clothes on," Carl said.

"Listen," Mick said. "We got an anonymous tip that something funny was going on here in this garage. Now that we know you live here, and you're not a thief, I'm sure you won't mind if we look around. Okay? Just stand over there by the garage door." Carl moved toward the door and Connor stood next to Carl.

"Strange that you turned the light off when you heard us coming," Mick said. "What, do you got car parts in here or something? Tools? I'll just take a look." He opened the top drawer of the workbench, which was filled with mismatched greasy tools and a random assortment of nuts and bolts. He opened the second drawer and saw the pipe and some wires. "Well, looky here. Looks like we struck gold. Don't look like car parts at all." Mick held the pipe up for Carl and Connor to see. "Does this look like a car part to you, Officer McManus?"

"Nothing like that for a car, no," Connor said. "But it looks like something I have seen before. That looks like the start of a pipe bomb." He glared at Carl.

"Come over here, Mr. Carl. Right now." Mick motioned and Connor moved Carl to the workbench.

"Look, I don't want any crap from you," Mick said as he pulled Carl close by the shirt. Carl could smell the toxic breath in his face. "You tell us right now why you have this and what you were going to use it for. The truth now. You best give us the whole story."

"Okay, okay, I promise," Carl said as Mick released his grip and took a step back. "It was for practice, a test, you know. One of these went off at a school near here, and I was just curious. That's all."

"Practice? There some kind of practice field around here?" Connor said.

"I was going to a forest preserve, in the woods, so no one would get hurt," Carl said.

"And if it worked, then what?" Mick said, sticking his finger deep into Carl's chest. "You're not just making this to blow up some trees. Now's when you tell me the whole story. And don't make me upset by lying to me. You won't like how I get when someone lies to me."

"I haven't lied to you," Carl said, moving back from Mick and crossing his arms. "I'm telling the truth. And I'm guessing, just guessing, that you two might have some sympathy with what I'm thinking."

"And what is that?" Connor said.

"This neighborhood is going to hell with all them coloreds moving in." Carl rubbed his hands together. "They're taking over and pushing us out. You know what I'm talking about."

"So, say we did have some sympathy," Mick said. "Where does the bomb fit in?"

"Well, look, for example," Carl said, "there's a colored preacher and his wife next door. I thought of using the bomb on his house—not to hurt them but to send a message by blowing up their house. But then I worried that I might hurt my own house. That's why I wanted to test this thing."

"And if it works too well?" Mick said.

"There's this other family across the street," Carl said, "I can't stand them. They get all cozy with this colored couple next door like they're best friends or something. They rub my nose in it. I'm thinking that I'd put a scare into the people across the street. Sends a message to back off before it gets worse. That's what I was thinking."

"And these people across the street. Have a name?" Mick said.

"Pedersen."

Mick lunged at Carl, punched him in the gut, and then lifted him off the ground and sat him on the workbench right on top of the pipe. Carl gasped for air.

"Look, you dumb piece of crap." Spit flew from Mick's mouth into Carl's face. "I may feel the same way you do about the neighborhood. But you're gonna get somebody killed. I can see you already burned your hands messing around in here."

"Wait a minute, whose side are you on?" Carl said.

"Not yours," Mick said. "See, here's the other thing, dumbass. That's my family. I'm related to the Pedersens." Carl's eyes grew wide. "Nobody messes with my family. And nobody, white or colored, should get hurt or killed or have their house blown up for what they think about their neighbors. Understand?" Mick thumped Carl's chest. "Get what I'm saying?"

Carl nodded and hung his head. He was about to apologize and plead for mercy when Mick lifted him off the pipe and the workbench and grabbed his shoulders.

"You hurt my family and I will hurt you," Mick said. "You really don't want to find out what that's like."

Carl looked toward Officer McManus, but he was looking out the garage window.

"I may not like colored people moving in here," Mick said, "but they're people. We're all people. Even you, you dumb turd. We gotta be able to live with each other."

Carl stood silently, looking at the floor.

"This is how it's gonna be. Listen up," Mick said. "We're taking this here pipe and wires and whatever else we find in here that don't go with a car. If we hear of a bomb going off anywhere around here, we're coming for you. More than that, if my nephew falls off his bicycle and skins his knee, I'm coming back here to beat the crap out of you. Don't make me do that. This stops here. Now. And the only thing you should do in that forest is go for a hike. Understand?" Mick grabbed Carl's collar and brought his face up to his. "DO YOU UNDERSTAND?"

"Yes, yes I do. You won't ever see me again, I promise," Carl stammered.

Mick slapped Carl across the face and then implanted his finger onto Carl's forehead. "Good. Now get your sorry ass back to bed before I change my mind and arrest you."

Mick escorted Carl outside, and Connor picked up the pipe and wires and scoured the garage for any more contraband. He found an old bag full of pamphlets from the Ku Klux Klan. "What an idiot," Connor mumbled as he stepped outside. Carl shuffled back into his house while Otis and Marvin crouched closer to each other, seeing the pipe had been recovered.

The squad car crept slowly away down the alley until Mick pulled over at the end of the block and turned to Officer McManus. "So tell me officer, just what did you see there in that garage tonight? Anything at all?"

"Well, Officer O'Rourke, I didn't see anything at all. Not one thing," McManus replied.

Mick paused a moment before saying, "Could you imagine the amount of paperwork and red tape involved if we did see anything?"

"Like I said, I didn't see anything."

"Right you are, sir," Mick O'Rourke said with a smile on his face. "Right you are!"

Twenty-Three

The Reverend Calvin Wolthuis knew the day was coming when his leadership of the Grace Christian Reformed Church would be defined forever. He knew he had to make a statement about what was happening in Englewood and about whether or not the church should leave. Over the past few months he'd wondered if he could avoid this by taking a call to another church—he even prayed that God would release him from his call to Grace—but it had been years since another congregation showed any interest in him, and he wasn't about to try and get the word out that he was available and sell himself like some cheap marketer. No, he was stuck in place, and this cup would not pass from him. The Reverend Wolthuis did not like conflict, and after serving Grace for twenty-two years he wanted to be comfortable, not courageous. He decided the wisest thing to do would be to go with the flow and find a way to justify the growing pressure to relocate the church. He would give his flock what they wanted.

Radical change was happening all around, and the Reverend Wolthuis did not like it one bit. He'd kept in touch with the seminarian Simon De Bolt after De Bolt's summer internship had ended and De Bolt gave the impression that the very seminary the Reverend Wolthuis had attended a few short decades earlier was now adrift in social concern. This sounded like liberalism, and the Reverend Wolthuis suspected the seminary appeared to be in danger of losing its moorings over issues that distracted from the church's vital gospel mission. De Bolt wrote that there was lively conversation at the seminary about the pressure Dr. Martin Luther King, Jr., had applied on President Kennedy to issue a second Emancipation Proclamation. This King, the Reverend Wolthuis thought, may be an articulate preacher and inspirational speaker, but he consistently oversteps his bounds. Much to the Reverend Wolthuis's disappointment, De Bolt himself appeared to be drifting. He'd written questioning whether some parts of his internship had been misguided and even went so far as to suggest King was a contemporary prophet in the tradition of Amos, Jeremiah, and Isaiah. This was a bridge too far, and the Reverend Wolthuis wrote a sharply worded letter warning De Bolt that not only was he on a slippery slope, the very future of his ministry was in jeopardy.

Once he'd sent his missive to De Bolt, the Reverend Wolthuis turned his attention to preparing the sermon of his life, the sermon that would define his career in the pulpit.

The text was from the Old Testament, Exodus 8:20. God tells Moses to confront Pharaoh and say, "Let my people go, so that they may worship me." This was exactly what the Reverend Wolthuis had been looking for. By tying together worship with leaving, the Bible gave theological justification to his pragmatic thinking.

Back in the days when the seminary was sound, the Reverend Wolthuis had been taught that a sermon had three points, preferably stated in alliterative sequence. He crafted this sermon, as with all of his sermons, to last about forty minutes. He always preached without a note in front of him, wearing a freshly pressed suit, a crisp white shirt, and polished black wingtips, his standard preaching uniform, which befit the solemnity of his sacred duty. This Sunday called for more, and the Reverend Wolthuis had also put on a vest.

When Sunday came, at the Reverend Wolthuis's request, the elders sat by themselves in the first row. The Reverend Wolthuis wanted their presence there to lend additional credibility to his words, to be a visible affirmation that the lay leadership of the church agreed with the Word of God delivered from the pulpit. It was not unheard of for the elders to sit in the front row to signify their supervision of the preaching of the Word and their role as guardians against heresy. Over the years, though, different elders had made it clear that they wanted to sit with their families. Not this Sunday: they filled the front row.

It had come to the Reverend Wolthuis as he prepared that the decision of the Englewood Christian School Association had made his path simpler. He couldn't imagine contradicting the will of the people so clearly articulated by the decision to move the school. As he sat in his study looking at Moses and Pharaoh and thinking about Englewood, his sermon took shape around these three points: Called to Leave, Committed to Worship, and Convinced of Renewal.

When he mounted the pulpit, the Reverend Wolthuis slowly surveyed the congregation without saying a word, even staring for a moment at those seated in the balcony, where some uneasy with the church tended to gravitate. Church balconies, in the Reverend Wolthuis's long experience, were filled with those who felt that doubt was not the same as unbelief, and teenagers congregating without parental supervision. As the Reverend Wolthuis scanned the pews, the measured silence captured the congregation. With a deep breath, he began to cast a vision for the future of this congregation, one which reflected the tea leaves he'd been reading for months.

> Brothers and Sisters, we read in the passage before us that God, through his chosen servant Moses, gave a clear, concise, and clarion call to leave the land of Egypt for something new, something fresh, something that comes with the blessings of his covenant promise. We, too, albeit centuries beyond that moment, share in that covenant promise. Today also, we hear a call to leave. But it is not enough to hear the call to leave, though hear it we must. We must also discern God's will at any given point in history as his people. We must hear his call and discern the time, detect God's meaning, and decide according to his eternal will. Today, as in the days of Moses, we must heed the entreaty, the overture, the Call to Leave!

Henk Koning and Mel Lamsma, sitting side by side in the front row, both felt reassurance and affirmation in their decision to move the Christian School. Many others who had been on the fence about moving felt themselves leaning. The very voice of God was saying it was time to leave Englewood. Even those who regularly tuned out the sermon sat on the edge of the wooden pews. They awaited the second point, which came on schedule thirteen minutes later:

> And not only must we hear and discern the Call to Leave. We must notice why it is we must leave. Scripture is crystal clear on this point. It leaves no doubt, no question, no query. We leave to worship! We are Committed to Worship. And, as we know—yet need to be continually reminded of—all of life is worship. It is not only when we gather here in God's house. We worship as we work. We worship as we rest on this Lord's Day from all that distracts from our devotion to our God. I ask you to search your

> hearts this day and answer this question: Does worry distract you from worship? Do you find your daily prayers and scripture readings more difficult these days compared to a month ago? A year ago?

Without a direct reference to what the faithful might be worrying about, the point was made. Fear and even hate were allowed to run freely throughout the church. Many reflected on the murder of milkman Fred DeVries, a member of this very congregation, a tragedy still fresh on everyone's mind.

The Reverend Wolthuis paused, dramatically flourished his handkerchief from his pocket, wiped his brow, and continued:

> This day, the Lord's Day, is unlike any other day, and we dare not participate in worldly activities when we can praise him with rest, pure rest, from the distractions and temptations of life. We also worship when we send our covenant children to our beloved Christian School as the glorious Heidelberg Catechism reminds us in Lord's Day 38, in the wonderful explanation of Sabbath rest, so that the ministry of the gospel and the schools are maintained.

And so the Reverend Wolthuis, for the next fifteen minutes, linked leaving and worship to the strong communal and inseparable bond of church and school, hinting not so subtly that one could not live without the other, and one may not leave without the other. In addition, his argument for leaving stood not only on scripture, but the very Heidelberg Catechism itself.

He wiped his brow again before continuing:

> And finally, Brothers and Sisters, it is not enough to hear the Call to Leave. It is not enough to Commit to Worship. We must notice from God's Word that if we hearken to his Call to Leave and Commit

> wholeheartedly to Worship, we must also be Convinced of Renewal. Imagine with me, if you will, the great opportunities we may have as a congregation in a new land, just as God called his people to a new land of his choosing. Make no mistake. God, through his servant Moses, called his people to a new land, a land of promise, flowing with milk and honey. And they acted in faith. One foot in front of the other, marching to Zion, beautiful, beautiful Zion.

Then the Reverend Wolthuis reached for his handkerchief and in a measured, theatrical movement wiped an imaginary tear from his eye.

> Leaving this neighborhood will not come easily. This I know. We have been richly blessed by God for many years in this community. We acknowledge, however, that Englewood is no longer our community. Things are changing all around us, at a speed none of us could have imagined. But we need not leave with regrets if we set our sights on the renewal that will come with God's blessing. Think of it! Think of life in a new promised land! Will you heed the call? The Call to Leave? Committed to Worship? Convinced of Renewal?

His final word was a hearty "Amen" and then the Reverend Wolthuis descended the pulpit to receive the handshakes from the elders, all of whom shook hands enthusiastically or clapped him on the shoulder while offering their own quiet "Amen!" All that is, except for three elders: Magnus Pedersen, Meine Decker, and Arnie Medema offered their hands and looked away in embarrassment.

Just before the close of the worship service, after the final hymn, and before the Reverend Wolthuis raised his hands in the posture of benediction, Michael Schaap walked quickly to the podium and whispered in the Reverend Wolthuis's ear, asking if he might say a few words to the congregation. It was an extraordinary moment, a rare breach of the liturgy for a congregation who took their cues from I Corinthians 14:40: "Let all things be done decently and in order." The Reverend Wolthuis nodded, motioned for the congregation to be seated, and retreated to one of the large wooden chairs behind the pulpit. All eyes were now on Schaap, the missionary aviator, standing before them in his American Sunday suit. "Brothers and Sisters," he said, "I, like you, am deeply moved by today's sermon." He paused, surveyed the congregation, settled his view on Ruth, Benjamin, and Naomi, and cleared his throat. The Reverend Wolthuis smiled at what he took to be high praise. "But perhaps not in the same way." He glanced in the direction of the Reverend Wolthuis, then addressed the congregation.

> I am an ambassador for the gospel of Jesus Christ and your representative to the people I serve. You give of your resources. You pray for our work and our well-being. You sent me to love the people of Nigeria, to live with them, learn from them, and live the good news with them. So, I ask you. Are dark-skinned people important to us only if they live thousands of miles away? If God's people fled Egypt because of Pharaoh, who is our Pharaoh today? Who is our enemy? Who is it that poses a threat? Black people who move uncomfortably close to us? Are we talking about moving our church and school because we can't live with or live near people with different colored skin?

Michael Schaap nervously ground his left shoe into the altar carpet. He glanced back toward the Reverend Wolthuis, who appeared to have his eyes shut in prayer. Schaap let his words sink in before he continued.

> I hear the conversations and the demeaning words. My children hear the same disgusting words at the school playground and don't know where to turn. People, these words are racist words from racist hearts, hearts that are bent and broken because they want to diminish people of a different race because we think ourselves superior, and they, inferior.

With this, Henk Koning and Mel Lamsma rose, turned their backs on Schaap, and walked down the center aisle, the only sound being the creak of the wooden floor as they left, motioning to their families to join them. The Lamsmas did. The Konings stayed put.

The Reverend Wolthuis rose and stepped toward Schaap, who held his hand up and said, "Just one more moment, please. I'm almost finished." The Reverend Wolthuis stepped back but did not sit down, feeling it was important for people to see this was still his church. Schaap continued.

> We don't have to move lock, stock, and barrel. You know I grew up in a congregation, in a church, that moved out of Englewood a few years ago. This doesn't have to happen here. Not again. We can make this work. We can welcome rather than run. Are we so afraid? Our Bible says repeatedly, 'Don't be afraid.' Yet I am afraid. Afraid that we are panicking. Afraid that we are unwilling to open ourselves to others unlike ourselves. Afraid of the message we send and the witness we make by moving.

He stopped and shook his head from side to side. "That's all. That's it. Thanks for listening."

As Michael Schaap returned to his family, his wife looked him in the eye and smiled, whispering to him something about what school was going to be like for Benjamin and Naomi tomorrow. The Reverend Wolthuis quickly offered the benediction and the organ blared the postlude as the congregation made for the doors and the sidewalk, eager to talk about what just happened. The three elders who had been indifferent to the Reverend Wolthuis's sermon, Magnus Pedersen, Meine Decker, and Arnie Medema lingered, seeking out Michael Schaap to shake his hand.

When he reached his home, the Reverend Wolthuis fielded five phone calls demanding the removal of financial support for Michael Schaap and his family. After another call, he left the phone out of its cradle so that anyone dialing would receive a busy signal. He had no stomach for Sunday dinner and suggested that he and his wife take a ride in the car to escape for a while. They backed down the driveway and headed for the southwestern suburbs. He wanted to see the future for himself.

Twenty-Four

Magnus and Fenna were not persuaded by the Reverend Calvin Wolthuis's Exodus sermon, but, then again, they found few of his sermons inspiring. That's not to say there were not things about their pastor they appreciated: He faithfully visited the sick and the widowed and brought them words of comfort. He made a sincere effort to know his congregation, their needs, and their dreams. When he led funeral services, they sensed that he truly knew the deceased. Yet, while he was keen on doctrine and delivered sermons with practiced eloquence, compassion and empathy rarely made an appearance in his ministry. More than that, they felt he took the easy way out with his Exodus sermon. He brought fluency but left courage behind.

Magnus and Fenna had admitted to each other long ago that they were not enamored with the God they found in Exodus either. As much as they both found the portions of the Bible about Jesus persuasive and comforting, especially when he spoke of loving your neighbor, they weren't sure what to make of the God they found in places in the Old Testament. The God of Exodus not only freed his people from the perils of slavery in Egypt, he then drowned Pharaoh and the Egyptian army in the process. That didn't sound like loving your neighbor. They only voiced their scriptural misgivings to each other and wouldn't dream of bringing them up at church, but they found the Reverend Wolthuis's justification of leaving their beloved neighborhood by using a problematic Old Testament story objectionable. When they spoke of their sermon qualms later that afternoon, Fenna suggested that maybe a good person to talk over the Exodus story with would be Willowby Jackson. Sadly, that conversation never happened.

Magnus and Fenna were in the small number of those at Grace Christian Reformed Church not swayed by the Reverend Wolthuis's Exodus sermon. His provocative permission to pull up stakes was all it took for many congregants to sense divine approval for their decisions to sell and move. It seemed to Magnus and Fenna there was a palpable perverse pride in many of their fellow church members, who now had ecclesiastical affirmation that their instincts had been right all along. They didn't need to examine their fear and unease around Black people. They didn't need to ask themselves if they simply hated another race. They could move without guilt or remorse, for they'd been told that God had called them to leave.

Magnus and Fenna had been moved by what Michael Schaap said, yet as the Pedersens left church that Sunday morning, they overheard groups of congregants speaking with outrage about Schaap's words. Magnus didn't know what to say when Henk Koning said, "I'd buy him and his family tickets back to Nigeria if they'd leave now." He overheard others saying Schaap's words were only natural, given whom he'd married. Magnus and Fenna felt Schaap's remarks were an accurate assessment of the struggle and choices in front of them, and worth considering. But they knew Schaap's was a voice calling in the wilderness.

A few days after the Exodus sermon, on a warm fall evening, Magnus and Fenna took their kitchen chairs out to the front porch after their kids were in bed. "We've danced around it long enough," Magnus said. "We're going to need to make a decision." He looked across the street and gave a wave to Michael and Gabriel, ever vigilant at their posts.

"Here's what I'm wrestling with," Fenna said. "If we stay and the church and school move, where does that leave us? The kids will have to start over at a new school, and we have no idea what that means. What will be left of the world they know here?" Magnus leaned back and listened. "If we stay," she said, "and decide to drive out to the suburbs multiple times a week for school and church, I have no doubt that we'll be shunned and shamed."

"You're probably right," Magnus said. "I never thought about the shunning, but I suppose that's a possibility. I can think of a few who'd happily turn their backs on us."

"It seems to me," Fenna said, "that we're going to be starting over whether we leave or stay." They both looked out at the empty street a while before Magnus spoke.

"It's more than starting over," he said. "We have to think about this financially. I ran the numbers on my lunch hour the other day, and it isn't pretty. Everyone I've talked to who has sold says the same thing: they didn't get what they expected for their house."

"We can learn to live on a tighter budget," Fenna said. "We've done that before. I'm not so worried about money. Here's what I'm really losing sleep over: I don't want to move. But if we stay, will the kids be safe? George Clement still haunts me, let alone Fred DeVries. I couldn't live with myself if something happened to the kids."

That night on the porch, Magnus and Fenna made the most difficult and painful decision of their marriage. Their conversation wound on for some time, with each taking turns presenting arguments for and against moving. Eyebrows were gently raised in the dark, and objections were quietly considered. As with their neighbors and fellow church members, in the end, fear won out. For Magnus, it was fear of financial disaster if they stayed. For Fenna, it was fear for the safety of their children. All around them, fear had spread like a virus, and they weren't left untouched. Moving seemed the safest thing to do.

Over the coming weeks and months, they were approached by numerous realtors. Sometimes the realtors simply wanted to buy their house. Others offered to help them sell it. One was quick to point out that in a very short time, their block would be one-third Black.

It was a jolt. A few years earlier, buying their brick bungalow on Green Street after living in an apartment had been both a reward for their frugality and a move of extravagance. Many homes in Englewood were wood and frame, spacious enough but not like the sturdy construction of brick. Their house said they had arrived, that their years of hard work and thrift had been rewarded. When they first moved in, they imagined they would grow old with each other on Green Street.

When they were ready to sell, Mel Lamsma handled the transaction, and the final offer stunned them. They would receive enough to pay off their mortgage, but would have to start over financially.

The Pedersens had never owned a car. Magnus took public transportation to work and everything else they needed was in walking distance in the neighborhood. At Thanksgiving dinner, Magnus announced he'd borrowed the Medemas' car so they could go for a ride the next day. He didn't say a word about researching a potential move, just that it would be fun to go for a drive. The next day the Pedersens climbed into that car and headed to the southwest suburbs, to see for themselves the areas under discussion by the church and school as likely sites for relocation. Neither Erik nor Kristen had the heart to ask if this meant they were going to move.

Some of the neighborhoods looked like Englewood and most of Chicago, with the streets laid out block by block in a grid. Other neighborhoods had curved streets and old, tall trees. The more recent suburbs didn't have trees, just newly planted saplings fresh from a nursery.

Erik felt out of place. The houses were far apart, separated by driveways that led to garages. There were no gangways, where you could stretch your arms and touch your neighbor's house. There were no alleys behind the houses, which meant there was no place to play catch or climb a garage roof without being discovered. School was out of session for the holiday, but he didn't see any kids, even in the small playgrounds scattered around. He didn't see anybody out in a yard playing touch football or at a park shooting baskets.

It took a while, but eventually Erik figured out what bothered him most about the houses. There weren't any front porches in the suburbs. There were small cement stoops in some places, but more often you walked right up to a front door and into a house. How could you have a home without a front porch? It was the place where life centered, where families gathered, where you listened to White Sox games and police calls, where you waved to friends and neighbors, and cooled off on hot summer nights.

After a while, Magnus drove to the proposed lots for the school and the church. Both sites were spacious and overgrown with weeds and scrub bushes. If you didn't know this was progress, you'd simply think the places were deserted. It was Kristen who said, "Looks like *Little House on the Prairie*."

"Without the house," her brother said. The whole area was empty and quiet. There wasn't life all around, like in Englewood. Nor did they see any Black faces the entire time they drove. The area was as white as a bar of Ivory soap, which prided itself on being 99 and 44/100% pure.

After a while, Kristen asked, "How do people in the suburbs get their knives sharpened?"

"What?" Magnus said.

"Or scissors," Erik added.

"What are you two talking about?" their mother asked.

"The knife and scissor man comes down the alley with his machine," Kristen said. "There aren't any alleys here."

"People figure these things out," Magnus said.

"I don't want to figure it out," Kristen said. "I like our alley."

It wasn't until April that Magnus and Fenna broke the news to Erik and Kristen that they were going to move. To the many questions raised at supper that night, which were all variations of "Why?", the answer was: "You have to trust us. We know what is best. You'll see someday." After a while, Kristen stood, slammed her napkin onto the table, and then slammed her bedroom door. Erik sat wordless, head bowed, fighting back tears. Eventually he rose, went out the back door, and climbed into the tree house, where no one could see or touch him. His eyes scanned the familiar alley and looked out toward the National Tea parking lot. Cars went up and down Halsted, just like they did every day. Nothing was different. Englewood was the same as it always was. Why did they have to move? His parents, especially his father, his hero, had let him down. Erik expected more from Magnus.

Magnus and Fenna grew more distant after the announcement, preoccupied, and absorbed with the many details of moving. Silences engulfed the family as resentment and anger grew. The kids felt powerless and never could have imagined their parents felt the same way. Magnus and Fenna couldn't resist the multi-headed dragon that was compelling them to move. They were sure they were right, but being right didn't help them feel any better.

Moving day came in May, and the day before the truck arrived Magnus and Fenna made sure they did two things. First, the whole family walked across the street to say goodbye to the Jacksons. After that, they walked through every room of the Green Street bungalow, telling stories and sharing memories, bringing a sense of closure to the reality of leaving this place that had been such an integral part of their lives. Each of them felt, but did not fully have words for, how much Englewood, Green Street, and this house mattered to them.

Willowby Jackson said many nice things to Erik and Kristen, but his parting words were addressed to Magnus and Fenna and had a bit of a sting: "For a long time, I have thought that you white folks were immigrants to Chicago and us Black folks were refugees. I don't think that's right anymore. Now I think you and your people are nomads. My hunch is that you aren't done moving. History has a way of repeating itself. You'll uproot and move again once some folks with dark skin move to the suburbs. But that's just my hunch. In any case, Godspeed and God bless!" Then there were hugs all around on the Jacksons' front porch and even Sheila wiped a tear away.

The family tour of the house provided a brief respite and a sense of comfort in the sharing of memories. Magnus made fun of the hours he had spent on his "throne," admitting that he was actually smoking in the bathroom after dinner each night. Fenna stood at the kitchen sink recalling the time some new neighbors who lived in an apartment down the block came for supper and reprimanded Erik and Kristen for mishandling the dishes while drying them. "Never touch the wet dishes with your hands," Fenna quoted them. "Only the dish towel should touch them."

Kristen said she'd miss the roller-skating parties in the basement, skating in one circular direction around pillars, the furnace, and the porcelain washing machine with the hand wringer. Erik brought them into his bedroom and talked about being terrorized as a little kid by the stairwell leading to the attic. He said that he used to imagine monsters descending upon him down the creaky stairs.

The moving truck came at noon the next day. They had not yet purchased a home—they couldn't afford a down payment and had just bought a used car, a necessity in the suburbs. They had rented an apartment in Oak Lawn.

The moving company was the same one Old Man Finnegan had used, and Erik recognized the same large man with a cigar clenched in his teeth when he spilled out of the truck and ambled up the sidewalk.

Erik stood alone on the porch with his hands in his pockets. "Aren't you the same guys who moved the man two doors down a while ago?"

The man leaned back. "Yeah, kid, you're right. That would be us. Do your parents want us here or around back? Find out, wouldja?"

Before Erik turned to find the answer, he said, "Do you remember if that guy, Mr. Finnegan, had a shotgun by the front door?"

The man laughed hard and said, "No, no shotgun. Looked to me like a machine gun. Ask your old man where he wants us."

Erik and Kristen sat in their customary places on the porch, out of the way of the movers who had parked their truck in the alley. Erik thought of all the time on that porch with the Green Street Boys. He hoped maybe Frank or Eddie might come by, but they didn't. Frank was on duty as an altar boy for the Saturday afternoon Mass. Eddie stayed home, worried that if he came over he'd cry. Pete Koning's family had already moved. Turns out Pete's aunt and uncle weren't the only ones scouting out a new location. They were out of Englewood by Easter.

Erik was looking up the street toward Eddie's house when a Chicago police squad car pulled up. Uncle Mick stepped out, put on his cap, adjusted his belt and the gun strapped around his waist, and approached Erik and Kristen.

"I need to talk to your folks," he said.

Erik and Kristen both scrambled into the house to find their parents and stayed inside listening while Magnus and Fenna went to talk to Mick on the porch.

"So, I'm cruising up and down and see this moving truck in the alley," Mick said. "What's the big secret? I didn't hear you were moving." It was true. They hadn't told all their relatives yet.

"It don't matter," Mick said. "We never saw things eye-to-eye. But I thought I'd at least stop and see. And tell you this: I told you so months ago. I bet you lost your shirt for waitin'." And as Mick gave a dismissive smirk and turned toward his patrol car, he mumbled to himself, yet loud enough for all to hear, "Clueless. Just clueless. Save their house if not their lives and still they have no idea." Shaking his head and laughing, he waddled to his squad car.

By four o'clock, the truck was packed and the movers were ready to head to the apartment. Magnus and Fenna walked through the empty bungalow and swept the floors one last time, Erik and Kristen sat on the front porch until Erik said, "I'll be right back," and walked down the gangway to the backyard.

Magnus and Fenna held hands in the living room, and Magnus unsuccessfully fought back tears while praying, "Good and gracious God. We bow our heads in gratitude for your blessings here in this place. Guide us now, in your mercy, as we go into the unknown. And keep Willowby and Sheila Jackson in your gracious care. In the name of Jesus, we pray, Amen."

They locked the front door and then asked Kristen where Erik had gone. She shrugged and nodded toward the backyard.

Magnus walked back and found Erik in the notch of the maple tree in the treehouse he'd built years ago. The treehouse had always been the place Erik retreated to, the place where he met heroes in books and comics. Robin Hood. Jim Hawkins. Tom Sawyer. Huck Finn. Atticus Finch. The Flash. Even Batman.

Erik thought of those stories. Huck had saved Jim. Or maybe it was Jim who saved Huck. Batman saved Gotham City over and over. Robin Hood saved Nottingham. But Atticus Finch couldn't save Tom Robinson. He thought of the day George Clement had been beaten and pictured his mom waving a spatula and his dad throwing his briefcase into the stomach of one of the attackers. After a minute, he realized he was looking over at the second story porch where he used to see Doris Eck. The Ecks were long gone, and Erik didn't know where they'd moved.

"Erik," Magnus said from the ground. "It's time to go, son."

A plane bound for Midway roared overhead while Erik slowly climbed from his perch and down the slats nailed to the tree for steps. He stepped in front of Magnus, turned, and took a long look at the alley before saying, "Dad, what if Mr. Clement hadn't been beaten up?"

Magnus sighed. "Erik, I don't know. That's a good question for another time. I'm afraid it's time to go now." Erik took a step and Magnus stopped him. "You know," Magnus said, "I sometimes wonder the same thing." Then they walked together down the gangway to the front of the house, where Fenna and Kristen waited by the car.

A moment later, Erik stood with his family at the curb. They looked at each other, and then looked around, soaking in the last images of home and neighborhood, the sounds of traffic from Halsted Street, and the sight of fresh growth on the trees.

Willowby and Sheila were on their porch. With uplifted arms, Willowby raised his voice. "May the Lord bless you and keep you. May he make his face to shine upon you. May God lift up his countenance upon you, and give you his peace."

There was no one on the Bensema porch. A For Sale sign was planted in the parkway. They would be among the last whites to move from this section of Green Street.

Before Erik opened the door to the back seat for Kristen, something Magnus noticed with a smile, he took one last look north, absorbing the homes of his approaching memories. Doris Eck. Old Man Finnegan. George and Millie Clement. He then looked one by one at the houses of the Green Street Boys: Pete Koning, Eddie Medema, Frank Bertolli. Erik thought of each, and their quirks and many adventures together. He turned and looked back at the porch where they had always congregated. Choking back tears, he whispered, "Goodbye."

Author's Note

This is a fictionalized account of events from my childhood on Green Street in Englewood. Real events, like riding in my Irish uncle's Chicago police car, or a church hiring a seminary intern to track where Black families were moving into the neighborhood, are mixed with fictional events and characters to give a sense of the dynamics at play. My research included Chicago newspapers and church council and Christian school board minutes.

Racism and racially motivated violence are facts, not fiction, and played a significant role in every changing Chicago neighborhood in the early 1960s.

This account from WMAQ NBC Chicago News in 2013 gives insight into the changes in Chicago broadly, and Englewood specifically:

> What's most striking about Chicago's pattern of racial distribution is the almost total absence of whites in Black neighborhoods. Even the city's whitest neighborhoods—Mount Greenwood and Lincoln Park—have Black populations of 4.7% and 4.9%,

respectively. But of the 28 neighborhoods with Black majorities, most have white populations under 2%. The absolute most racially polarized neighborhood in Chicago is Englewood, which is 98.5% Black, 0.6 percent white and 0.4 percent Latino. Of Englewood's 35,186 residents, 34,658 are Black, 211 are white, and 141 are Latino. In the 1950s, Englewood was mostly German, Swedish, and Irish. They've all gone, leaving only a Lutheran church.

From 1960 to 1980, Englewood's white population 'plummeted from 51,583 to 818,' according to the *Chicago Reporter's* history of the neighborhood. Not even ethnic cleansing in the Balkans achieved the levels of turnover that white flight in Chicago did.

For Further Reading

Linda Gartz, *Redlined: A Memoir of Race, Change, and Fractured Community in 1960s Chicago* (She Writes Press, 2018).

Henry Louis Gates, Jr., *The Black Church: This Is Our Story, This Is Our Song* (Penguin Press, 2021).

Kenneth T. Jackson, *The Ku Klux Klan in the City, 1915-1930* (Ivan R. Dee, 1992).

Christopher H. Meehan, *Growing Pains: How Racial Struggles Changed a Church and School* (Wm. B. Eerdmans Publishing Co., 2017).

Natalie Y. Moore, *The South Side: A Portrait of Chicago and American Segregation* (St. Martin's Press, 2016).

Mark T. Mulder, *Shades of White Flight: Evangelical Congregations and Urban Departure* (Rutgers University Press, 2015).

Beryl Satter, *Family Properties: How the Struggle Over Race and Real Estate Transformed Chicago and Urban America* (Picador, 2009).

Robert P. Swierenga, *Dutch Chicago: A History of the Hollanders in the Windy City* (Wm. B. Eerdmans Publishing Co., 2002).

Acknowledgments

The gestation period for this small novel was nearly a lifetime, if one considers having lived through much of its story and now being decades removed from it. It wasn't until the 1980s, when I expressed the desire to write something, that my wife, Cathy, who died of cancer in 2015, encouraged me to start the process, suggesting the form of a memoir. After early experiments seemed less than satisfying, drafts of opening chapters in novel format shared with friend Jeff Carpenter and colleague Dan Diephouse affirmed the change in genre.

Along the way, I reflected on a research paper I co-authored with Ron Nydam while attending Calvin Theological Seminary. We studied the movement of churches and Christian schools from the racially changing Englewood and Roseland neighborhoods of Chicago to outlying suburbs. That research uncovered systemic efforts in real estate practices and governmental policies designed to keep Blacks from moving into white neighborhoods. We also uncovered documents from church councils and school board minutes which reflected veiled and outright racist attitudes. All of this was to become part of the atmosphere of this novel.

A turning point came with my participation at a Scriptoria Conference, a workshop for aspiring writers co-sponsored by Calvin University, Aquinas College, and Cornerstone University. A chapter of the novel was workshopped under the guidance of the Canadian novelist Hugh Cook. I received the affirmation I needed from my classmates and Hugh to complete the novel. Hugh would later provide wise and insightful editing suggestions, as did author and friend Caryn Rivadeneira, whose enthusiasm was contagious.

I never envisioned at the outset that a novel is a communal effort. Many became involved in the process, for which I am deeply grateful. Lou Sytsma brought his knowledge of White Sox history. Mark Hiskes persuaded me that I was writing a story that should be told. Rick Williams gave me insights into the dynamics of race relations, as did Dr. Ted Williams III, Reggie Smith, and Dr. Robert Price. Lifelong friends Ron Lavery and Betty Deckinga Vander Laan experienced many of the forces described in the novel and gave helpful feedback. My sister Karen Merchant shared memories along the way. My pastor, Roger Nelson, a master preacher and storyteller, inspired me in affirming the "arc of justice," which is the telos of all creation. Our children and their spouses found ways to encourage me with their interest in the project and responses to earlier drafts.

Editor Jeff Munroe and I spent many hours on Zoom calls. I looked forward to each one. His blend of humor, insight, suggestions, and sheer interest in the subject matter and time period shaped this novel for the better. Jeff's attention to detail and historical accuracy, especially when it came to baseball, was a wonder to behold. The fact that we shared a similar faith tradition and hope for the future made the editing process a pleasure rather than a burden.

And then there is Sally, my wife. Combination cheerleader, queen of the commas, and savvy sensor of tone and character and conflict, she was always interested in the project and supportive of the time it took to complete. An avid reader, her suggestions always resonated with my hopes for the novel. Couldn't have done it without her. Thanks, Luv!

About the Author

Dave Larsen is a native Chicagoan, having spent most of his life living in or near Chicago. His interests include the history and architecture of Chicago, kayaking the Chicago river and area lakes, writing and storytelling. A regular contributor to the *Reformed Journal,* Dave has also published articles and reviews in *The Banner, Think Christian,* and *Christian Scholars Review.* Dave earned a doctorate in Educational Leadership and Policy Studies from the Loyola University of Chicago, a Master of Religious Education degree from Trinity Evangelical Divinity School, and a Bachelor of Arts in English from Calvin University. Until his retirement, he was the Executive Director of the Bright Promise Fund for Urban Christian Education in Chicago. His faith development as a Christian was nurtured primarily in the teachings and neighborhood of the Reformed tradition. He came to a deeper appreciation of the Roman Catholic and Mennonite justice traditions through his graduate work. He and his wife Sally live in a delightful, racially diverse southern suburb of Chicago. Together they have five married children and eleven grandchildren.

Connect With Dave Larsen

Thank you for reading *Green Street in Black and White*. If you enjoyed this book, and think that others would find it helpful, please leave a review on Amazon or on Goodreads.com.

A discussion guide is available at reformedjournal.com/books.

Dave Larsen is available to speak to your church, community group, or be a guest on your podcast. Contact Dave Larsen at: GreenStreetInBlackWhite@gmail.com.

You can connect with Dave on these social media sites:

Facebook: bit.ly/DaveLarsen

LinkedIn: LinkedIn.com/in/david-larsen-8692b24

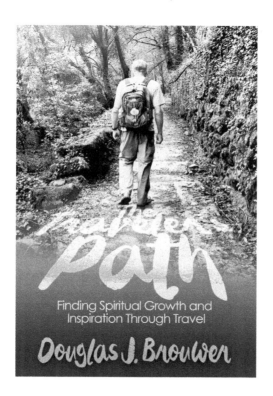

www.ingramcontent.com/pod-product-compliance
Lightning Source LLC
LaVergne TN
LVHW040855210325
806483LV00005B/9
9781641802161